Gauntlet

The Phoenix Cycle: Book One

by John G. Doyle

*This book is dedicated to my wife and
that devoted BFF. You all know who you are.*

Prologue

I might be dead in a few hours.

Please, I don't need your pity, sympathy or any other means of giving me the old pick me up gig because, honestly, I think I'm way past the dealing with death issue.

My only regret is that, if I do happen to die soon, it won't be from natural causes, I can assure you. Which bites, really, because I bet a tired old doctor would've just loved to have had a patient that was almost ok with dying.

Just saying.

So, now that we've all established my demise and, hopefully, are alright with the fact that you're about to hear a story by someone about to kick off and leave all his fans behind to wonder just where he's gone, then we can proceed.

I've learned many things in my travels.

Like how you should never buy food from certain vendors in Chinatown. Or that when in Rome, make sure you act as American as possible. I've learned how to defend myself, physically and psychologically, in many ways. I also have a knack for knowing how to dress no matter where I go.

Knowing these aforementioned items is nice and most certainly comes in handy every single day.

But there are some things that only I know. These *things*, as I so eloquently put it, mainly have to do with history.

Some of them aren't mentioned in the books, though. For instance, history books won't tell you that Vikings think a man in an expensive black business suit is perfectly normal, whereas the crusading English knights find it appalling.

The books tell us of the glory of chain mail and how it was the most ingenious idea of the Third century but also fail to let us know that you had to be able to bench press a jeep to be able to wear the stuff. Not to mention that it really didn't take off as the 'must have' armor until around the Sixth century and even that was really just in the Middle East. Don't ask because I just know.

We all know the three-hundred Spartans were a rough and tough group of handsome rogues bent on saving their culture with their supreme combat abilities. Of course we all do. Because of our precious history books and history channel. When in reality there had been almost fourteen-hundred of them. They did, miraculously enough, get their red loin cloths right, but forgot to mention just how uncomfortable they were. Not to wear, though, just the whole 'running into primeval combat in my underwear' thing. We all speak of their bravery, and for good reason, too. Going into a fight involving spears, swords, and other old school sharp objects, basically naked, is not for the faint of heart. I can tell you that first hand.

They told us Poe was a drunk crazy man. Wrong. They said Bonaparte didn't take over the whole world, when in fact the only places he didn't control in his reign were the undiscovered regions we now call the arctic.

History as we know it is wrong about everything. And not just about the sword and shield days, either. I'm talking about Marilyn Monroe, John Dillinger, and Joseph Stalin. Real recent type jazz.

I can't tell you everything. Mainly because I'm not supposed to know myself. Indeed, the knowledge I have and the way I acquired it is extremely bad for my health. But I've been quiet for too long.

So, sit down. No, really, you need to sit down for this, seriously.

My name is Jericho Johnson. I'm twenty-two years old, hate Irish wolfhounds with a passion and can swing a mean battle-axe.

This story begins in 793 A.D. I had just bought a new suit, it was raining and I had foolishly forgotten my umbrella.

Chapter 1

"Stupid, stupid," I muttered to my drenched self. The rain wasn't super hard but terribly cold. "Of course I remembered my camera but not my flipping umbrella."

I glanced down the hill and saw a band of fur-clad men approaching me. There were twelve of them in all.

I couldn't resist a quick snapshot of the dozen Viking warriors coming up the hill. Their axes and broadswords glinted from my flash as they came to a stop in front of me.

"Evening, guys. How are things?" I said to them, putting on my best smile and extending my left hand to the one who seemed to be the leader of the pack. I know that the right hand was the one most commonly employed for greetings among most all cultures, but due to the odd glove I had on my right, I decided the left would feel less aggressive.

I had been observing their small village for almost two days now. From a safe distance, of course, and only taking photos when the urge was too great not to obey. The man looked at my hand then at my black suit. After seeing that the guy was just going to leave me hanging, I put my hand back down.

Then he rattled off something in Scandinavian. Ah. How could I have forgotten? I guess because I hadn't actually had a verbal exchange with any of them since my arrival almost three days ago. I held up my gloved hand and hit a button. "What are your theories on global warming and the mad cow disease?"

This was the question I asked most of the time now. I used to amuse myself from time to time by seriously abusing the fact that the person I was speaking to didn't understand a single word I was saying. I ceased this dangerous practice because of one occasion in the late 1720s when I rattled out a very off-color insult to a man on the streets of Bruges thinking that he didn't speak English. Why did I think he wouldn't speak English? You guessed it. History books. My black eye certainly proved them wrong on *that* one.

The Viking before me now looked at his comrades for help and seemed a bit unsure of himself. Then he started talking. I listened intently, nodding now and then as if I understood.

A soft orange light blinked on one side of the glove for about thirty seconds before turning blue and glowing steady, indicating that my glove had obtained enough Scandinavian dialogue to put together their alphabet. "Show time," I muttered to myself, tapping an icon on the glove's screen.

"Now, what were you saying?" I asked.

The dozen or so Vikings in front of me went all sorts of wide eyed.

"How can you speak our language, stranger?" the man who had given me enough dialogue for my glove asked.

I thought about spinning some insane tale but thought better of it. "Does it matter all that much?" I asked instead.

"It does," was his reply.

I sighed. "Well, if you simply must know, it has to do with this glove," I said, tapping the said glove with a finger. "Or maybe you guys call these things gauntlets."

I frowned when I said this and gave my glove a long glance. The more I looked the more I realized that it really was more of a gauntlet than a glove.

"So," I said. "What'd you say your name was?"

"Bulwark the mighty, Bjourn the Berserker's younger brother," the one who had been doing all the talking said. He didn't seem the least bit puffed up about it, either. I know if I had a severely bodacious name like Bulwark the mighty or Bjourn the Berserker I'd pretty much wear a t-shirt letting everyone know about it.

"Well then, Bulwark, you guys have nothing to fear of me. I'm simply a man on a quest for knowledge. Nothing more," I said, smiling reassuringly at him. "I just want to know about your people. Your likes, dislikes, if you guys really have braided beards..." I glanced over the lot of men in front of me, just to make sure one of them was sporting one of the sweet beards I always gave my Dungeons & Dragons character. None of them were.

Of course, what I was telling them was true depending on how you looked at it. "Bjourn is not welcoming to strangers," Bulwark stated almost awkwardly.

"Would you mind letting me meet Bjourn?" I asked. This was a shot in the dark. The odds of these people letting some weirdo stranger have an audience with their chieftain wasn't looking too good. But one of the things I have learned in my travels is that the worst thing they could do was tell me no.

Or decapitate me.

Bulwark pondered on this. "Do you have any weapons, traveler?" he asked this cautious enough, almost as if he were afraid I was a wizard and could be offended or something. His eyes dropped to my gloved hand. Not that I blamed him. The fingers on it were thick at the base and ended in some devilishly sharp points.

I chose my next words carefully. "No axes or swords to speak of, Bulwark," I said, extending my hands palm-upward to allow them all a good look. "This glove is just for traveling," I said and one of the Vikings on my right narrowed his eyes. Seeing that he was toting a wicked cool hammer, I added, "And no hammers."

Seemingly satisfied that I wasn't packing, Bulwark simply nodded once and turned to head back down the hill toward the village.

I was relieved that swords and shields were the standard weapons of the time so they didn't have cause to give me a thorough once-over because, as it happens, I was indeed packing.

It was all about the gauntlet. Apart from having the capability of sailing me through time and space and looking totally awesome whilst doing so, it dueled as my weapon/defense against unfriendly characters. I didn't know all the ins and outs of it, but I had gotten the hang of the important bits.

I'd had it for a little over a year at the time, but the fact that it was extremely futuristic technology and that I just skimmed through the digital manual on the glove like a lame birthday card from my Aunt Greta were both key factors in why I wasn't completely familiar with all the glove's capabilities.

Sure I'd tested out all the buttons in a secure location. Which, incidentally, was the Arabian Desert in 1894, where I was sure no one would get hurt. After messing around with it for a few hours, I had deduced that If you took away the bells and whistles from the glove, you know, like that thing called time-travel, it was basically a future hot shot, except the electricity shot out in a visible bolt that went out around thirty feet and could probably knock someone at least that far if I had to use it on anyone. It also had something my nerd-mind wasn't quite ready for.

A grappling hook.

Back then I didn't realize just how useful one of those could be, but I sure do now.

There was a screen on the top of the wrist part that showed me basically everything a time-traveler should know. Like the date at the top left-hand corner and the temperature at the top right-hand corner. It was a little over twenty degrees when I was with the Vikings. The rest of the screen was mostly taken up by little important tidbits such as my heart rate, oxygen level, and blood pressure.

One button at the top center was labeled "weapons/defense," and the other button to the right of that one said "new date" and was where I put in the date of the next place I fancied visiting. Example: if I put in Paris, France, 1645 and hit enter, I would be there in less than fifteen seconds. I know. Wicked, right?

When we reached the village, the rest of its inhabitants stared at me all wide-eyed. I didn't get a chance to find out why because their chief met me at the front door.

"What is it you want?" he bellowed, brandishing a bodacious double-bladed axe that looked like it weighed more than I did. "Speak, outsider."

In my year of traveling, I had encountered more people like Bjourn the Berserker than I could count. Afraid of the unknown. Handling them was not always easy, and I could see already that the exchange with Bjourn was sizing up to be a nasty one if I didn't play my cards right.

"Chief Bjourn, I trust?" I said, noticing to my delight that his blood red beard was braided into two neat rows that reached his stomach. "My name is Jericho Johnson," I said, dipping into a small bow. "I have come from a very long way to see the might of your dynasty and to see if all I've heard of you and your valiant warriors were true."

This was true. I had come there to see if Vikings were all they were cracked up to be and to check out the braided beard situation. But they didn't need to know that.

Bjourn narrowed his eyes at me, flicking them down to my glove. "And what is it that you have heard?"

Time to turn up that classic Jericho charm.

"Why, you have not heard the devastatingly beautiful dramas of Bjourn the Berserker and his band of Vikings?" I asked, looking very aghast that he hadn't.

Bjourn closed the gap between us. After he had stopped right in front of me and stared at me for an uncomfortably long time, he finally smiled and slapped me on the shoulder. "Well then, Jericho Johnson, you shall dine with us tonight in my great hall and tell us all of these tales about myself," he said, laughing.

After I had received a few more slaps on the back, I began realizing why they all wore armor. These guys could kill you with kindness. Bjourn then insisted on having a guide show me around his lands while we waited for the feast to be prepared. I was told that the feast would be ready in an hour and that the great horn would be blown when it was time.

Upon my request, I was granted some authentic Viking garb complete with a pointed helmet and about five wolves worth of furs. PETA would've had a major field day with these dudes.

I was most excited to discover my guide to be a gorgeous warrior woman with white blonde hair and a mean looking sword slung across her back. Some of my excitement was due to the fact that history had only had a few speculations about Viking women being warriors, but let me be completely honest and say that most of it was because she was absolutely smoking hot.

"You are the traveler?" she asked me, sounding as if she'd rather be having her right arm slowly sawed off instead of having to show me the sights.

"Name's Jericho," I said. "And you are?"

"Piper."

"Where?" I said, looking around for some 8th century instrument player.

"No, fool, my name is Piper."

Wow. A Viking warrior-chick named Piper?

It was probably a good thing she didn't have a name like Arwin or Gwendolyn because I'm pretty sure my inner nerd would've taken over and I would have tried to kiss her, or something.

We started our journey at the village square where she showed me the fish market and then the tanner and blacksmith. I was working my digital camera overtime and it had started drawing her attention.

Piper had been silent the whole time I was snapping photos like a wild man, but I could feel her eyes on me. "And what, in the name of Odin, is that?" she asked, peering at it curiously.

"This is Thelma," I said, handing her my camera.

She examined it curiously. "But what does it do?"

This was always fun. "Here," I said, taking it back. "I could show you faster than I could explain it."

I stepped back from her and held it up so I could see the pretty Norse girl on the camera's screen.

"Say cheese," I said.

She blinked at me for a few seconds before she finally caught on that I really did want her to say cheese. "Uh, cheese?" she said before the flash went off and she almost shouted, "Thor's beard!" before instantly looking around to make sure none of the older folks had heard her blasphemous comment against the god of thunder.

Teenagers. I guess they weren't really that different over a thousand years ago, after all. "Sorry. I probably should've warned you about the flash," I said, turning the camera around so the shaken girl could get a look at herself on the screen.

She stared open-mouthed at the photo with unbelieving eyes. "How does it work?"

"I know it's a lot to take in but there isn't a super computer in the world that can do what your eyes do in a few fractured seconds. Come on Pipe, smile. Whatever you're doing when I push the button on top you'll be doing on this little screen back here."

She smiled big, showing her white teeth and I forgot to take a photo because I gawked at her like an idiot. In any movie about the old school sword and shield days, they always give the female protagonist, or antagonist for that matter, perfectly white teeth even though we all know that they had zero help with keeping their teeth clean, right?

"Why are you looking at me that way?" Piper asked, breaking my concentration on the serious breakthrough.

I blinked and shook my head a little. "Sorry, Pipe. You just have really nice, uh, teeth," I said, sinking further into the mire of my own idiocy.

"Thank you," she said, nodding politely. "You have nice teeth, too."

"Thanks, sweetheart. The Colgate must be working."

Her eyes widened and her mouth fell open. "You've been to the Coal Gate?" she asked this with a mixture of wonder and fear.

I frowned. "The what?"

"The Coal Gate," she said, dropping her voice to a whisper

and leaning in toward me. She smelled kind of like cinnamon. Just thought you should know that. "It is located north of here. The entrance is hidden but it is said to be the gateway to the underworld."

Oh, right. *That* Coal Gate. The entrance to Hel's frozen front porch, so to speak.

I thought about telling her I had been to Helheim and back just to see the kind of street-cred that sort of venture gave a guy in the 720s, but I thought better of it.

"Actually, Piper, where I come from Colgate is the name of something that cleans our teeth."

It took me a good ten minutes to convince her that, no, I had never been to Helheim and that I was really telling the truth about toothpaste. Just when I had finished up my lecture on Colgate we heard the great horn blow, indicating it was chowtime.

Oh well. I suppose I could finish sightseeing the next day. I still had a while before my college students back in Chicago had to turn in their mid-term exam papers, but none of that mattered considering I could just zip back to exactly when I left.

Because, you know, time-travel.

But another thing that I've learned in my travels is that making plans and time-traveling mix about as good as oil and water.

Of course, back then I had absolutely no idea that there was a completely insane psychopath bent on world domination that also wanted me dead so he could have the gauntlet.

Nope. I didn't find out that crazy revelation for another two whole days. In actual time, though, because I stayed with the Vikings for a while before heading home.

So, cut me a break, whoever-you-are. Because, like I just said, how the Helheim was I supposed to know?

Chapter 2

"So, can anyone tell me where Emperor Nero went wrong?" I asked the seventy students seated in the auditorium.

Silence. Not that I blamed anyone. Defending Nero about, well, anything wasn't easy.

And, just in case you've forgotten already, there aren't very many twenty-two-year-old college professors. Almost half of my class was made up of people around twenty to twenty-two. The rest being the kids who did well enough in high-school to make it to my classroom before their nineteenth birthday. I know. God bless America, right? Some kids actually did graduate. There also was the occasional thirty- to forty-something men and women deciding to better their education later in life. If I had to choose between these few classes of students and pick the hardest to teach to, I would have to go with the older folks. Mainly because most of them aren't keen about the idea of their professor being almost twenty years younger than them.

I leaned back in my desk chair, placing my laced fingers on top of my head and tried not to sigh. "Look, guys, we all know about Nero being this horrible emperor. But can anyone in this room please tell me at least one good thing that he did?"

I pointed to the first hand that went up.

"Mona, if you please," I said to the bright-eyed brunette sitting on the front row.

"If he would have been proven guilty of setting Rome on fire, then he would also be responsible for getting more land available to the southern farmers and increasing Rome's reach into the grain industry," Mona said, adjusting her glasses.

I didn't think she would've even thought of that. "That is, oddly enough, the most satisfying answer I've received all day. Thank you, Mona."

Of course, being a history teacher with the ability to travel back in time, Nero had been one of the first historical figures I had tracked down. I had already proven that he was, in fact, accountable for the great fire. Mona's stating Nero's one good accomplishment had been dead on. Had the fire not happened, the fall of Rome would have happened almost two-hundred years earlier than it did by my calculations.

Oh, and incidentally, Roman historian Edward Gibbon was right. It did happen in A.D. 476, just not on September 4th. It was sometime in late June.

Also, I will never want to meet Nero again. Ever.

I talked a few more minutes about how Rome was, even with all its wanton and bloodthirsty ways, one of the greatest civilizations to date. When the bell rang and everyone started standing, I reminded them about an essay that was due by late next week and bid them all a warm journey home. Speaking of home, that's where I couldn't wait to be.

Chapter 3

I dropped my bags, coats, and briefcase on the foyer floor. This was my ritual every time I stepped into my condo. "Hi, honey, I'm home!" I called cheerfully.

The journey home had been uneventful. I'd stopped by a coffee shop close to my house to do some boring paperwork but had decided to finish up later after I'd gotten my real work done concerning time-travel.

Evonne Mitchells, butler extraordinaire, appeared on the scene. A butler was one of the first things I added to the twelve-thousand square-foot condo that, as I like to look at it, was more of a mansion than a condo, complete with a spiral staircase, tennis court, and inside pool.

"Ah, Master Johnson. I trust you had a pleasant day?" he said, stooping to retrieve my coat.

"Let Louise get that, Mitch," I said. "I need you in the basement stat."

"I have given Miss Louise the night off," Evonne said, dropping my coat over his arms and straightening. "She had a hard cough and needed time to recuperate, sir."

I nodded and stooped to pick up the backpack and briefcase I'd just thrown down. "Billionaires having to pick up their own luggage off the vestibule floor," I shook my head. "What's the world coming to, Mitch?"

"I am sure I do not know, sir," he said.

"Come on, Mitch, lighten up. We've got a lot of planning still left to do tonight."

"Of course, sir," Evonne said. "I took the liberty of having Owen pick up your favorite tacos from downtown LA and they are in route. The estimated time of arrival of your private jet is exactly thirty-eight minutes."

"Awesome, Mitch. You're the best butler-with-a-Britishaccent ever," I said, patting him on the shoulder. Sushi tacos. No one did it better than downtown LA.

We deposited my coats and bags in the enormous closet to the left of the front door and headed into the enormous living room. Although, when you own a house this huge, the area that is generally called the living room is the boasting room. The best view, fireplace, expensive furniture, water fountain with naked angels adorning it. You know the drill. The walls were also laden with weapons from almost every age imaginable.

Come to think of it, I've never even sat in the boasting room. But sitting would have to wait. We crossed the fancy room to the door that led to the elevator. The door opened to a short hallway that eventually ended at the elevator that went down five stories to the basement/lab.

I pushed the level five button and stepped inside. "Come down when my tacos get here, please."

"Of course, Master Johnson."

Then the doors closed.

Evonne was a retired captain of the military that had gone secret service that had gone hitman that had finally gone butler. But aside from having such an amazing life as that, Evonne Mitchells had one specific characteristic that made him invaluable and irreplaceable in my eyes: an unreasonable love of history.

The weekly combat/weapons training that had begun with his arrival was also fun. It was kind of cool to have your teacher refer to you as master, too.

He was also one of two people from 2012 who knew about my knack for traveling back in time. Tonight was extremely special for Evonne, though. He didn't know it yet, but I had finally decided to ask him to join me again, on my upcoming voyage.

He'd come with me only once before when I'd gone to see Nero and, I've got to be honest, that little venture didn't end well.

The elevator dinged again, and the door opened to a ten-foot hall. The floor, walls, and ceiling were all made from chrome steel. At the end of the short hall was yet another door that required my hand impression, retinal scan, and voice recognition for access. After slapping my hand on the scanner, widening my right eye, and saying my name, the one-foot-thick steel door slowly opened from the ground up.

I walked in and clapped my hands twice. The lab was where I spent most of my time in the house. Upon my clapping, the enormous room lit up with white lights.

"Welcome, Jericho Johnson," a female computer voice announced when I entered. As much as I'd like to say that I had an artificial intelligence that I could talk to and would do all my paperwork for me, that would be a lie. I had the female greeting installed with the lab. I mean, why not, right?

Inlaid in the walls were some touchscreens that reached the floor. Right now each one of the six-foot-tall by ten-foot-wide screens were all filled to the brim with my Rome information. The first had longitudes, latitudes, and some of the most accurate maps I could find of A.D. 97 Rome. The second had names of famous structures, places, and people of that particular date.

The tops of most of the tables in the room were the same touchscreen monitors, just laying down. These were easier to access so were employed in basically all my studies. A private lab had always been a dream of mine, but since I was now a celebrity, I realized that normal things normal people get away with couldn't apply if I wanted to keep my extracurricular activities under wraps and away from the public eye.

Like being able to just plug into the same internet everyone else was using. No, that wasn't a good idea because WikiLeaks had been wanting to debunk me from the start. So I did what every billionaire does when they need some parts of their search history covered beneath the clandestine.

I bought a satellite. Several, actually, to maintain my link continuously when one of my expensive hunks of space metal decided to do what it was designed to do and orbit away from me.

The tables that weren't boasting the touchscreen tops were located at the back wall and were all overflowing with armor and weapons from at least twelve different eras. I approached these and selected my latest edition. The double-bladed axe that Bjourn the Berserker had his best blacksmiths craft for me before my departure yesterday.

I'd swung it around for a few minutes when I heard Evonne's voice buzz over the speakers. "Your sushi tacos, sir."

"Admit guest," I said, and the steel door slid open. Evonne stepped in with a tray held high. He brought it over to the table with a three-dimensional map of the entire city of Rome glowing green from the monitor and set it right on the coliseum.

"Your tacos, sir."

"To work, then," I said, diving onto the platter of sushi tacos and relishing the first bite.

After a few hours of sifting through all the information we had about A.D. 97, me crunching merrily away on my tacos and Evonne doing most of the work, my butler proposed the brilliant idea of going back to A.D. 98 instead. "Cornelius Tacitus, Roman historian and senator, finished two whole books that year, Master Johnson. And Emperor Nerva died and was succeeded by Trajan."

"Think I could get my hands on those books?" I asked, licking my fingers after swallowing the last of my tacos.

"Possibly. And the celebration for a new emperor would not be one to miss, sir," he said, swiping his hand over the screen to scroll through his list of events. "Trajan also went to Germania the same year and defeated the Bructeri, returning as a hero. What a busy little emperor. Yet another glorious celebration."

I had mapped out my landing spot in the city, choosing some grassy flats on the outskirts. What? Did you think I would blindly appear somewhere in the great city of Rome? No. Not a good idea. My glove could just land me anywhere but would land me in exact places when the correct longitudes/latitudes were punched in. "We need to grab the books last so we can zap back to Chicago if we have to steal them," I said this purposely and watched Evonne's reaction.

He had his back to me but turned his head slightly. "Master Johnson, did you say *we*?"

I smiled and walked to his table. "I did indeed, Mitch," I slapped him gently on the shoulder. "I need a hand on this one and, who knows, maybe we'll get to use all that combat training you've been pouring into my head."

He nodded simply, as if I had just asked him to ride with me across town instead of time and space. Then he added, "I hope we do not have to use any combat training whatsoever, Master Johnson. Rome is not the best place to have a good knowledge of such things, sir, and after Nero..."

"Yeah, yeah, I remember Nero."

I walked to the bulletproof glass case that held my white metallic glove, spinning on a turnstile like a show car. "Well then," I said, taking the glove out and slipping in on my right hand, wincing a little as the tiny jolt of electricity hummed on the veins in my wrist. Within a few seconds my heart rate and temperature appeared on the screen. "We'll just have to nip that it the bud, now won't we?" I said, pointing a ridiculously sharp finger at the coliseum.

Chapter 4

The roar of the seventy-thousand Roman citizens was deafening. Literally. Evonne and I blended in well wearing our scholarly robes in the upper section of the coliseum. No one noticed us as we both produced a pair of earplugs and put them in. Not that they helped that much, but at least our eardrums didn't feel like they were about to burst.

And they said rock music was the number one damaging thing for ears. I'm guessing whoever came up with that statistic had never watched a bloodbath unfold in a coliseum filled with eager, bloodthirsty Romans.

As we watched the scene unfold before us and the body count started to rise—or drop would be a better term—the more men that fell let the viewers know that their entertainment was almost at an end, and it made me somewhat proud to be an American.

Obtaining money in such places was never easy, and Rome had been no exception. After wasting two precious hours at the market and doing a little jumping back a day or two, Evonne and I had been handed enough money to purchase almost everything we needed for our expedition by a few truly perplexed merchants. Our buys mainly consisted of robes and sandals. I pocketed the remaining denarii and set out for the arena, with Evonne close behind.

Getting in wasn't hard after a quick cash flash and a comment about the two of us being part of the senate; we were ushered to some of the best seats to watch the sport.

I mean, if that's what you want to call it.

Let me just go on record here to say this: blood and sand mix a little too well. For real. After a few minutes the hot sun coupled with the hot sand results in a large dark brown spot that's usually accompanied by the body of some poor shmuck who has just given his last breath, all for the sake of entertainment.

So am I proud to be an American? Yes. Yes, I am.

I glanced over at Evonne and noticed that he was watching the spectacle with a shockingly cavalier attitude about the whole thing. Then I remembered that he used to be a major league black ops dude. No doubt he's seen stuff almost this bad. Maybe even worse. This wasn't the case for me, and I was beginning to regret my rashness in coming to the arena at all. Don't get me wrong, my travels haven't left me unscathed, and yes, I have seen folks killed.

The crusades were rough times. Too rough to explain in a few pages in a history book. I had stayed in the Holy Land almost the whole first month after getting my glove. I became a squire the first day and was working for a good-natured Englishman by the name of Sir Rodney of London. The real article, that guy was. From London and everything. After he'd taught me the basics of swordplay for a few weeks, our camp was attacked by raiders.

Please try and understand that I am a twenty-two-year-old almost billionaire with severe fanboy-like tendencies.

So at the first shouts of an attack, I'd run out of my tent shirtless and brandishing my claymore and red-crossed shield. I discovered that my glove had a grip like a crocodile's jaws as I clenched the hilt of my broadsword and waited for the oncoming enemies.

I totally blame my inner nerd for the two lives I took that night. Had I been thinking clearly, I would've just zapped back to the windy city at the first signs of attackers. But I hadn't been thinking at all, much less clearly.

Watching the blood hit the sand now and turning my head away just before the inevitable decapitation of the sod on his knees clutching at the deep stomach wound that had just been issued by the beheader, I recalled the surreal, primeval feeling that had gripped me that night and had been the cause for my sword swinging true twice.

Upon arriving back to Chicago the next day, I had sworn to

myself not to be so foolish again. Will I defend myself if someone is trying to hurt me? Yes. Will I kill someone I meet in my travels if they're trying to kill me? Not if I can help it.

The crowd started shouting louder, if that was even possible, to the winning gladiator to not end it too quickly. At least that's what I gathered due to the immense theatricality the victorious gladiator was flaunting to the maniacal crowd. He put a hand to his ear as if he couldn't hear what they were screaming at him then nodded knowingly after a few seconds. He knew exactly what they wanted.

He rolled his neck once before swinging at the man's throat, hitting the jugular vein. I didn't need my earpiece in to know what the audience had been shouting. This was what the crowd came to see. Not just death. That wasn't good enough for them.

But shockingly visceral, mega-bloody, all-out-gore was what they wanted.

I turned my attention to anywhere else but the scene before me, not caring to see the winner who was probably holding his arms up to receive the bloody shower that no doubt was already happening due to the reaction from the spectators.

Somehow, I kept thinking that violent video games should have prepared me for this. But they didn't. This made God of War look like Winnie the Pooh.

"Master Johnson, it seems the match is over," Evonne shouted next to my ear to be heard over the roar of onlookers. "Perhaps we should make ourselves scarce."

Upon exiting the arena, we headed west, roughly in the direction of the house of the senate, if the map on my glove was correct. The passing people were all talking about the last match. It resembled the way teens talk about how amazing a movie they had just seen was as they exited a theater. This notion was increased due to the teens we saw swinging imaginary swords at one another and talking about the highlights of the arena.

Side note: Rome is pretty much the most amazing place I've ever traveled to. Coming from the guy who has personally watched the first stone of the Great Wall of China being laid into place and witnessed the birth and execution of Charles I, in the same day, might I add.

But, seriously, Rome was beautiful. I never really worried about people seeing my glove in my travels. I mean, yes, it is the most advanced gadget probably ever invented so far, but I never had anyone try and lift it. Good thing for them, too.

Oh, yeah. I guess this is probably the best time to tell you that the glove I keep going on about wasn't exactly made in 2012. Yes. This is the best time to tell you that. Is it the best time to tell you when, exactly, it was made and how I, the genius prodigy who graduated college with a master's degree in history at the age of twenty-two had come to obtain it? Not so much.

Suffice it to say that I'll tell you about all that later. Maybe. And you can stop with the judgmental thoughts because, contrary to the viewpoints of a few characters you haven't met yet, I didn't steal it.

The streets were packed with Roman citizens going about their Romany ways doing whatever it is that Romans happened to be doing at that time of a day in the great city of Rome.

Did I mention that I was in Rome?

It was A.D. 98 on a beautiful Thursday afternoon.

The day my perfect time-traveling life completely was dropped in the toilet. The day I finally met her.

I should have been more alert, I guess. I mean, when I look back on it I can see that I really should have been paying more attention to my surroundings. I'm also guessing that you know now that whatever horrible shenanigan my butler and I got into on that fine Thursday afternoon in A.D. 98 didn't cost us our lives because I've just told you that I learned a good life lesson from the experience.

No, we didn't die. But I still to this day don't know how.

Chapter 5

We had walked for almost five minutes when the beginning of my end took place.

"Master Johnson," Evonne said, placing a hand on my shoulder.

"What's up, Mitch?"

He nodded ahead of us and I glanced around, scanning the moving crowd. That's when I first saw her. Maybe it was because she was the only person in the crowd who seemed to be watching us. Or it could have been that she was paler than most of the tanned citizens. Her jet-black hair, perhaps?

But I'm thinking it was mostly because she was wearing a black, leather, long-sleeved jumpsuit with black boots that reached her knees. She was also walking straight toward us.

"This doesn't bode well," I said, stating the obvious.

"What should we do, Master Johnson?"

Like I said before, we almost died that day. Mostly because I, yes, I just said that, was too stupid not to see danger when it was swaying up to me in black heeled boots

"Let's see what she wants, Mitch," I said, dropping my voice lower. "Keep your guard up, though."

She came to a stop in front of us and looked us both up and down. "Jericho Johnson," she said, sounding like a villainess that has finally met her nemesis.

"That's me," I said, smiling. "Nice outfit, by the way."

She returned the smile, and I must confess, she was beautiful. In a kind of looks-like-she-could-kill-you-with-a-phone-cord kind of way. Her smile wasn't pleasant, though. It was the classic I-know-more-than-you type of smile.

"How has Rome treated you thus far, Mr. Johnson? Been to the arena?" she asked with an odd amount of malice and calm, and to my puzzlement, I noticed she had a slight Russian accent.

"Please, call me Jericho," I said, my voice almost sarcastic. "This is my partner in time, Evonne Mitchells. Now, how can we help you?"

"You find yourself clever, no?" she said, consulting her glove.

Wait, what?

Yeah, she had a gauntlet like mine. It was black and on her left hand, but it was the same every other way.

"Nice setup, lady," I said, looking at the glove and glancing at mine. "You find yours, too?"

"I did not steal mine as you did, if that's what you mean."

I opened my mouth to tell her I hadn't stolen my gauntlet of time but suddenly felt like I was being pulled over by some time cop, and for some reason it really got under my skin.

"So, how long is this going to take?" I asked in a bored tone. I could feel Mitch behind me coiled tight, ready for anything, and I was glad he was there.

"Which part?" she asked, closing out whatever she was leafing through on her glove and looking at me, her head cocked a little to the side. "Me taking back what you stole or me having to hurt you to get it?"

"Yeah, that's not going to happen," I said. "If that's all you're offering then I bid you a good day. Go try the mice on a stick a few streets over. I promise you won't be disappointed."

I tried to step past her, but she got back in my way quickly.

"I don't think you understand exactly what I'm saying to you," she said. "Let me try again." I heard the unholy hum emanating from her glove and knew that she probably had the same weapons/defense systems that I did.

And she probably had actually read that digital manual.

"I was ordered to retrieve the glove from you at any cost. Your life means nothing."

"Hey," I said, looking super excited and beaming at her while holding up a gloved finger. "Here's an idea."

Then she was out cold on the cobblestones. What? She, like, threatened my life, man. You think I have a problem punching some psycho-chick's lights out after she basically says she's going to kill me? Not hardly.

"Times up, Mitch," I said sadly, stepping over the mystery woman's crumpled body. "I hear the windy city calling our names."

"She could follow us, sir," Evonne said. "She does have the capability."

After a few brief moments of thought I said, "Alright. I know what to do."

Chapter 6

Of course I couldn't just zap back to my mansion in Chicago. No, that would've been too easy for me and also for whoever psycho-chick happened to be working for. So after Evonne and I had ducked between two large structures, I punched in a date and hit enter. Then I grabbed Evonne's shoulder and watched his feet begin to vanish.

My feet were also disappearing, this being what always started going first. It took a good ten to fifteen seconds for our whole bodies to slip from Rome.

Let me point out that I have never, to this day, let the feeling of jumping from one time to another become common to me. Especially when we jump from a good eighty-degree weather into an almost freezing climate.

The weather was what changed mostly because we hadn't jumped to another place but simply just another time.

The Holy Roman Empire, year of our Lord, 1228. Right at the start of the Sixth Crusade which was led by Frederick II, Holy Roman Emperor and quite the troublemaker. Well, not really led, because it took him years to get off his lazy butt and actually accompany the troops he had sent.

He did most of his crusading back about eight years ago during the Fifth Crusade, but currently he was also at diplomatic war with the papacy. Big no-no for a Roman Emperor, let me tell you. The date of his actual coronation was 1220, but he was really leading the country before that.

The streets were covered with snow as we made our way across it, shivering in our white robes. "What is the date, Master Johnson?" Evonne inquired while trying to keep his teeth from chattering.

"Late Ja-January, 1228," I told him, trying, to no avail, might I add, to keep my own teeth from clacking together.

"Come on, Mi-Mitch. Pull yourself t-t-together," I somehow, at the time, found our current situation extremely hilarious and began laughing as we walked along the white streets.

"I've been dr-dreaming of a wh-white Italy," I crooned through my drumming teeth while smiling like a maniac. "Not far now, Mitchy. I know a guy we can get some gear from. And if a guard happens to ask you anything about the Emperor, be sure to answer him back that the pope was right to excommunicate him again and totally rocks for it. Should keep us out of a cell with the other insurgents."

Evonne nodded. Not that I needed to remind him that the good Frederick II had actually been excommunicated on four different occasions and was even referred to as the antichrist by Pope Gregory IX.

The streets were pretty much deserted. Good thing, too. I forgot that after the riots, due to the second or possibly the third excommunication, a curfew had started. So after ducking behind abandoned carts and into dark alleyways to avoid the patrols, we reached our destination.

Our safe haven.

A semi-small hovel right off the street. Though it was late, even by partying Chicago standards, the place was bustling with activity. The only window flickered brightly from the many candles and considerably large fireplace.

I had discovered a long time ago just how very safe taverns were. I mean, these lowlife places had it all, man. Not only that, but it seems that the only thing that has changed since the first caveman bar is the installment of a television somewhere in the 1900s. But the overall atmosphere hasn't changed one bit.

"You cheat!" screamed a man, leaping up from his chair at a table and pulling a dagger. "I will cut your tongue out."

See? Later on down the road they'll be threatening the same thing about the TV.

Evonne was right behind me as we entered the warm tavern. I'll go ahead and let you know that we stuck out like a sore thumb. Two guys wearing senate robes, in the middle of winter, walking into the un-holiest place this side of the holy city. Not only that, but there hadn't been a senate in over twenty years or so.

"Evening, guys," I said, giving them all a little wave. "We robbed these from a couple of shmucks by the south gate. Get a load of these things," I added while grabbing a handful of white to show the bunch. This seemed to do the trick because the whole lot of them fell over laughing and sir dagger-a-lot even put away his weapon with a smile.

Evonne and I received slaps on the back all the way to the bar where a smirking man who was missing his left eye and a couple of fingers stood behind it wiping what was left of his hands with a rag.

"Jericho, Jericho," he said, still smirking. "To what do I owe this honor?"

I sat on a stool and exchanged fist-bumps with him. "You know me, Seth. I was just in the neighborhood and thought I'd drop by and see how things were getting along on your end of the world."

Seth smiled, then cut his eye at Evonne who had just sat next to me. After a second or two of inspection he raised an eyebrow at me.

"He's with me," I reassured him. "Evonne, meet Seth. The one-eyed, seven-fingered phenomenon of the Roman empire."

Seth bowed dramatically. "At your service."

Evonne nodded grimly. "Charmed."

"Ignore him, Seth," I said. "He's a tad nervous right now. What with all the riots and curfews and whatnot."

"Yes, it seems our liege has gone and got himself cast out by the church once again," Seth chuckled. "So what kind of trouble are you in this time, boy?"

"Hey," I said. "One, don't call me boy. Two, what makes you think I'm in trouble?"

The Roman's eye had a glint in it when he smiled. Poor lighting in the hovel, I was guessing. "Do you ever drop by for anything else?"

I watched him closely. "The Papal States need a little insight at times, buddy. Which brings me to the reason I pay you."

Seth shrugged that off. "I suppose. Follow me."

He lifted the bar entrance so we could follow him to the backdoor. A backdoor that led to a frozen walkway, which led to a snow-covered cabin-like object, which we entered.

The one-eyed man lit a candle. "Sorry for the cold. Had I known you were going to be spying right in the middle of complete anarchy I would have lit the fire."

"No worries, Seth," I said, rubbing my hands together and ignoring the man's sarcasm. "We'll need some new clothes as well."

"Swords?"

"A battle-axe would suit me better. If you can't find a good one, a gladius will do. With a wooden handle, though, not that ivory junk. Evonne will have the longest sword that these short-sword-loving Romans have around here." Seth was nodding, making mental notes.

"No shields, then?"

"Maybe if you guys didn't use shields the size of a Hummer."

Seth gave me a confused look. "I meant the size of a chariot."

"Well, they are rather large."

"I know. We'll make do without them."

Seth left us in the cold shack to go collect our list. We ended up both sitting close to the candle, holding our hands next to the flame. Not that it warmed us any but it made us feel better all the same. I took this time to explain our standings in the Year of our Lord, 1228. We were spies for the Papal States and Seth was our traitor accomplice who was aiding our goals. I had started this charade a while back and returned every so often, mainly just to check up on Seth, but the whole medieval espionage life was quite fun to dabble in.

And to hide from crazy time-traveling women trying to

kill me.

It took Seth about two hours to grab our gear, of which, might I add, contained not one battle-axe. The one-eyed man apologized more than once for this and kept saying he hadn't seen a good axe in years. To which I pointed out that if the Papal States won the war, there would be battle-axes for all.

I tested the balance of my gladius. Romans. You never had to worry about the lack of glamour with these dudes. It was still a cool short sword to be sure, but the intricate carvings got a little old. Seth had somehow even managed to uproot a long broadsword from somewhere for Evonne.

"Had I known that you had such a variety of weaponry, I would've put an order in for a claymore or two," I muttered.

"Sorry, Jericho," Seth said, shrugging. "That was left by some traveler many years ago. Figured it'd do better service with you two than letting it rust in a corner."

The clothes he scored were black wool and pretty comfy, for wool, I mean. Once we shucked our robes and donned the new clothes, we said goodbye to Seth and departed with our new weapons in tow.

I know what you're thinking.

He said that he almost died on that day, didn't he? Where's all the bloody chaos, man?

See? Told you I knew what you were thinking. I am pleased to inform you that it never came down to bloody chaos just then. And by just then I mean making it back to the street and walking for almost five minutes to the city gates. No action to speak of in that peaceful, snow-covered walk.

Only after we exited the city did the bloody chaos hit.

And you thought you were hearing a kid's story.

Psycho-chick saw us before we saw her, if the crater in city gate the size of a watermelon was anything to go by. The blue streak of lightning tore the hole when it missed *my* melon by almost three feet.

Evonne dashed to my left, leaving me. Smart guy, that one. Thinking back on it, I could see that he was splitting up, hoping that two targets was better than one if you happened to be rooting for the said targets, that is. Of course, right then it took me a few seconds to get over the initial shock of my pal leaving me before I kicked into action.

I darted in the opposite direction and hit a button on my glove. So she wanted to play with electricity, huh? Psycho-chick was about thirty yards ahead of me when I swung my hand up to return fire. My bolt struck home. That is to say that it struck her, but she jerked up her own glove and my bolt was deflected off of… something. What was that some sort of force field?

Great. And just when I thought my day couldn't possibly get any worse.

"Cheater," I called automatically.

Psycho-chick laughed and snapped her gloved fingers. Sparks shot everywhere from the friction. "Where is your friend?"

I guess she figured that I wouldn't fire anymore bolts because she started glancing around looking for Evonne. Guess all of her research hadn't shown her how trigger happy we full-blooded Americans were. Shield or no, I wasn't about to just sit there. I rushed forward, firing a bolt and holding the blue stream on her stupid shield which she had thrown up.

Holding a steady flow of the blue electricity had a downside, I found out. The down being that, in the event that I were to hold the stream for more than twenty seconds, my glove would start smoking. Not a good sign at all.

The upside though is that I look totally wicked while doing it.

The Russian woman watched my mad dash, but I'm thinking she really couldn't do anything about it. Partly because, well, she *didn't* do anything about it and partly because of how mad she looked when I stopped the stream just before I barreled through her shield, which, might I add, wasn't designed to keep out loads of testosterone, adrenaline and pure awesome, into her.

When I say I went through her shield and my rushing

body hit her, I'm not saying I performed a beautiful hurricane kick to her face. Not saying that at all.

All thoughts of finesse abandoned, I leaned into my dash and planted my shoulder right into Psycho-chick's stomach. I also made a mental note never to tackle someone like that again because I'm pretty sure that we were both equally hurt in the whole ordeal.

Evonne had been planning some kind of sneak attack on her, or something, but to be honest, I think my kamikaze maneuver threw a monkey wrench in that whole plan. He found the two of us writhing on the ground in pain. Me clutching at my shoulder while Psycho-chick held her stomach with one hand and tried to hold up her gloved hand to attack. I was also starting to think she had on some kind of body armor because I was really aching after our bout.

Evonne Mitchells, being the ever-gentlemanly man that he was, planted a boot on her glove and crushed it into the snow. "Who are you working for?" he inquired.

Man, but that guy gets to the point. Not only that, but he was being pretty calm about that whole shenanigan. Don't get me wrong, I pride myself on being among the most cavalier of dudes but not when someone was trying to kill me. All my cavalierliness (yeah, pretty sure that's not a word) went out the emotional window when Psycho-chick showed up with all her threats to my well-being.

Summed up I guess you could say Jericho lost his cool for a few seconds.

"Yeah, who?" I shouted too loudly while I struggled to my feet, still holding my shoulder. "Tell them I want to put in an order for your annoying force field and body armor."

Psycho-chick glared up at me while she grabbed at Evonne's boot with her free hand. She wasn't trying to get away, so I'm thinking that human reflex was to blame. I also figured that if some ex-hitman had my hand smashed into the snow, I'd probably grab aimlessly, too.

"I'm not wearing body armor, fool," she muttered.

I decided then and there that a change of subject was in order. That's all I needed was my curiosity as to why her abs felt like a brick wall to be discussed in the freezing elements.

"Grab her, Mitch. Let's take her back to the safe house."

Chapter 7

"So," I began. "Let's just all take a step back and breathe." I took a deep breath, let it out, and then glanced at Evonne and Psycho-chick, wondering why they weren't following my lead.

After staring at them for too long, they both seemed to get the idea and took a deep breath themselves. "That's better, right? We all feeling good now?"

Evonne shrugged while Psycho-chick glared at me. I'm getting really tired of saying Psycho-chick so let me clear that part up.

"So, what's your name?" I asked her.

"What're you going to do, Jericho, Google me?"

I narrowed my eyes at the bound woman, who, upon closer inspection made whilst either tackling her or tying her hands behind her back, wasn't really a woman at all. Old enough to buy alcohol, I was thinking. But barely.

"Oh, I'm sorry. You somehow haven't realized that you're tied up and aren't in control anymore."

Sarcasm. That'll have the lady loving you, Mr. Johnson. Maybe if she hadn't been snippy first things would've been a tad different in our little discussion. Evonne and I decided that her glove needed to come off ASAP, so we removed it right after our tumble in the snow.

She didn't produce a knife or gun or anything, so I was hoping that maybe her precious glove was the only defense she had.

"So that's a no on your name?"

"Chloe."

"And you're, what, German, or something?"

I knew she was Russian but also knew Russians hated being mistaken as German and wasn't about to let her get an edge.

"I am Russian," Chloe confirmed.

"You sure?" I frowned. "German, Russian. Same thing, really, since your nationality doesn't concern me."

Chloe glared at me. Get used to hearing that because she glared a lot. "It should, considering Russia created the glove you've been using for your little joyrides through time."

No flipping way.

Wasn't really expecting that. Granted, I knew that whoever had invented it couldn't have been American. Not to sound unpatriotic, but Americans really just let other countries create the good stuff and then pounce on the idea. I could already see off-brand time-traveling gloves at Wal-Mart.

"Let me guess. It was your father who is dead now or something equally as lame and overdone," I shot back.

"You know nothing," she began, a smile coming to her lips. And not the good kind of smile, might I add. It was the kind that let you know whatever else the smiler had to say was something you probably didn't want to hear.

"You just do whatever you want and never tell yourself no. Anyone that's not you only comes into your mind when you have the inkling to show off. You are, without a doubt, one of the most self-centered, impulsive, unfeeling human beings I have ever encountered."

I hate to say that everything she said was pretty much true. But at the time, I really didn't feel like being lectured.

"That's just it, Chloe. You don't know me. We've known each other for about, oh," I glanced at the time on my glove, "four hours now, only had contact for, like, thirty minutes of that. So you can keep your life-lesson speeches for someone you've actually met before."

Evonne laid a hand on my shoulder. "Master Johnson."

Chloe's smile vanished halfway through my rant, but one side of her mouth twitched a little when I'd finished. She looked like whatever she was thinking about was either annoying, amusing, or both. "We've known each other a lot longer than that."

What?

That's when I took note of Evonne's hand. I glanced at him with a frown.

"Your class, sir."

Then it all came back. I closed the small gap between Chloe and me and reached for her face, turning it sideways. "Mona?" I asked, then instantly felt stupid. But of course she was Mona. Funny how a teacher as good with details could miss one of his students when all she did was lose her glasses and dye her hair.

"Just so you know," I said, taking a step back and pointing an accusing finger at the imposter. "If you don't kill me before I make it back to Chicago, I'm so failing you."

"Oh, please don't fail me, Mr. Johnson," she gasped, wide-eyed. "I just don't know what I'd do if my peers from the year 2340 found out I flunked 2012 history."

I cut my eyes at Evonne. "You wouldn't by any chance happen to have a gag of some kind on you, huh?"

The butler shook his head. "Not at the moment, Master Johnson."

"Will you please stop calling him that," Chloe decided to cut in, really making the whole no-gag situation that much more annoying.

"Listen, *Mona*," I said, glaring at her. Great. Now she had me glaring. "If I paid you almost a million dollars a year to drive my limo and change my sheets, you'd call me master, too. So zip it."

"I don't know," Chloe said with a cocked head. "I'd have to look at your sheets first."

"So what's to keep me from convincing my extremely devout insurgent homies that you're a traitor to their cause and require immediate termination?"

Chloe laughed at that, "What? You think you're the only one with *homies* in different eras?"

"I'd like to think so."

"You thinking is a recipe for disaster."

"Your face is a recipe for disaster."

Wow. Why am I even telling you this part? I mean, it really happened, but I just don't like me not being in control. Whatever. Details. It's all about the details. Remember that, whoever-you-are.

"You mentioned something about the year 23-something," I said, trying to steer back on track.

"2340."

"Yeah, that. Is that where you're from?"

"And why would I want to cooperate with you again?" she asked.

I sighed. Man, but this girl was tiring. "Look, if you promise not to kill me, I'll untie you. Partly because the ropes aren't distressing you but mainly so you'll answer a few questions."

Chloe eyed me for a few seconds. Then said, "And if I choose to not answer your questions?"

I shrugged. "I'm feeling generous so I might not take your glove with me when I split if you just answer my flipping questions."

That got her attention.

"Ask your questions," she said, sitting on the dirt floor.

"Start with whoever invented the gloves."

Chloe started braiding her black hair. "That's a statement."

I just stared at her. "Are you really serious right now?"

She laughed. "No. You're just funny when you get your feathers ruffled," she was halfway done with her hair when she actually started. "My father, Dr. Atrium Sparks, was the one who discovered the phenomenon. He spent a good part of his life searching for it and finally stumbled on it in 2335."

She pointed to my glove for emphasis. "Don't ask me what makes these things work. It's a long story and I don't want to go into it."

"I know what the outside is made of," I ventured. "Other than that, you know way more than I do."

"The glove you happened upon is the first of the only three in existence. A year after the glove's creation, my father decided that it could never fall into the wrong hands and made it vanish."

Chloe stopped her tale and looked at me. "Tell me truly— did you steal the glove from my father?"

The answer was no, I hadn't mugged her daddy and lifted the Rolex of time off him. But I wasn't sure that I wanted her to know that I was innocent just yet. "I guess that all depends on what future Russians define theft as."

Chloe looked at me blankly. Since she wasn't glaring I was starting to feel our relationship was smoothing out some. I mean, aside from her trying to kill me, and all. "Alright," I said to her. "You want the truth? Here it is," I patted my glove. "I found this little jewel inside a container made from hard plastic and lead buried in Arizona."

This was, as farfetched as it seemed, completely true. Chloe chewed on her lip in thought, looking ever the cutest while she did it. Geez. Assassin, Johnson. Crazy-psycho-hit-chick from the future, man.

"Near Flagstaff?" the Russian girl asked.

Now it was my turn to chew on my lip, except instead my mouth dropped open like an idiot. "Ye-yeah," I stammered, falling even more into the pit of idiocy. "How'd you, uh, know?"

Chloe simply shrugged. "Not much left of your country where I come from. Or when I come from, I suppose."

Apparently she was done until she saw my raised eyebrows. "I suppose this would be the best time to tell you that America as you know it will be abolished in 2076."

Yeah. Now was probably the best time for *that* little piece of info.

"After the California incident in 2017 your government was in shambles. To be honest, the rest of the world was surprised that the US made it to 2076 to start with."

I didn't ask what the California incident was. Mainly because I'm pretty sure I knew what happened. What? It's basically sitting on a sandbar that's infested with pipes full of high explosive gases, guys.

"So what does that have to do with Flagstaff?" I inquired.

"After your government finally collapsed, mother Russia moved in. I'll spare you all the details of the uprisings in 2200, World War IV in 2278, and the civil war that is happening in my time right now. Suffice it to say that a planet can only burn so many times, Jericho. Flagstaff, Arizona is one of the few remaining cities left in what was once America."

This was a lot to take in. Like, a severely large amount to take in.

"I'm surprised that you, with the gloves power, haven't ventured into the future. Why is that?"

I just shrugged, although it was true. From the moment I found my glove and started my expeditions in the past, I had made an unwritten, unannounced rule that traveling too far into the future was off limits. "Maybe I just wanted to leave the future to God," I said, trying to sound sarcastic but not pulling it off.

"Or maybe you're just afraid," she said, completely seeing through my entire fabricated persona. The same one that I'd been cultivating for years. "You're probably telling yourself that your travels are to prove history wrong. When in truth you're really going because you know what's coming. This is just a game to you and history itself is your walkthrough. The only thing you've ever feared is the unknown. Why else would you have started pushing yourself at such a young age to achieve knowledge? To you, knowing how to accomplish something is better than the accomplishment itself.

"You have to know what's coming, don't you," Chloe had long since lost her college girl attitude and had once again became the murderous Russian. "Tell me, Jericho," she said, leaning toward me. "Did you see me coming?"

Chapter 8

To say that I was speechless would be, in fact, a lie. Big one. I had lots of things to say to little miss Russia. But, in the end, all I ended up saying was for her to tell me more about why she was trying to kill me. That sounded like something that needed to be cleared up.

"Verde von Klaus."

I frowned. "Who has a clown?"

Chloe narrowed her eyes at me. Since this still wasn't a glare, I was starting to think maybe we were getting on the right foot for once. "Verde von Klaus is the name of the man who sent me."

"Oh," I nodded slowly. "So, I just need to go talk to him, then. Clear up this whole misunderstanding in a flash."

"Considering he sent me to kill you, yes, I'd say things would be cleared up in a flash at your meeting," said the Russian girl.

"So why the college girl ruse?" I asked her. "You've been in my class for years."

"Six months," Chloe corrected.

"Really?" I asked, frowning slightly. "Odd. You sure I haven't failed you a few times already?"

Chloe smiled at that before finally telling me what I wanted to know. "I had to find out if you even had the glove in the first place."

So much for being the picture of carefulness. Upon my stating this, Chloe suddenly burst out in peals of laughter. "So the future predicting, all-knowing, history loving billionaire was careful?" After she got the reigns pulled back on her funny horse she said, "The people of your time were easy to fool because they know nothing of true suffering. Sure, America has had their share of sticky situations, but in the end they always came out on top. Now they're presented with someone who can, to them, predict the future. Should they embrace this newfound superman, or pick apart every detail to find out what's really going on because, of course, men aren't capable of feats such as these?"

I couldn't answer that, which I guess was what Chloe wanted because apparently she wasn't finished.

"Have you ever heard of the butterfly effect?"

"Of course," I answered. "I hated all three endings of that movie."

"It was rather odd, I'd say," Evonne threw in.

Chloe rolled her eyes.

"Yes, I know about your theory that relates to trampling innocent insects. What's your point?"

"My point," Chloe said. "Is that on one of these field trips of yours, sooner or later, you are going to mess up something big."

Man, she really wasn't going to like what I was about to say.

"I tested that theory. Didn't pan out," I said casually.

"What have you done?" she asked, aghast.

Shrugging, I said, "Not much. Punched Da Vinci' in the face, made sure that a certain emperor didn't have a fiddle when Rome burnt. Easy stuff."

After looking at me for what seemed like a long time, Chloe said, "And?"

I shrugged again. "And nothing. That's just it. Nothing happened differently."

"That doesn't make any sense," she said, looking confused for the first time.

"Not really, when you think about it," I told her. "We've all just been looking at time the wrong way. Instead of the past being this ever flowing life stream that makes the future possible, it's just the past. Look at it like time takes a picture every millisecond, when we go back in time it's like stepping on a painted sidewalk. Our presence on the sidewalk doesn't change the painting, neither does whatever we do while we're there."

Chloe had been listening to this intently, which I was thinking was a good sign. "So I guess what I'm really trying to ask is, since you and I now know that your butterfly theory is a bust, what's the *real* reason you're trying to kill me?"

"I don't have to kill you. I just need the glove."

I watched her brows furrow in thought as she chewed at her lip a little. After doing this for too long, she finally said, "I told you your glove was unique, yes?"

I shook my head. "You said there were two others and that was pretty much it."

"The glove you found was the first my father created." she said. "He tried to keep its existence secret but since the whole operation was funded by Klaus, it was only a matter of time before he found out."

Then it all started making sense. Or, about as much sense as a crazy story like this could, anyway. "So your dad hid it in the past somewhere near Flagstaff."

"Exactly. The construction of the second glove was just for that purpose alone."

"Wait. Hold up," I told her. "You're saying that your old man built a whole other glove just to hide this one in the past?"

Chloe stood and Evonne bristled slightly, a hand flying to his broadsword. "Easy, Mitch," I said to him.

"The first glove possesses two important things that its cousins lack," Chloe said simply. "I can only make one jump in a twelve-hour period with mine; whereas, you can change times every few seconds should you choose."

I frowned, examining my glove. "No kidding?"

"Not only that but the first glove is also the only one of the three capable of transporting others simply by touch, whether you are taking them with you or bringing them back."

I stopped checking out my gauntlet of time long enough to give her a horrified look. "Bring them back? Like, people from the past to the present?"

She nodded.

Wow. I had never in my wildest and most crazy ideas that

had to do with time-travel even considered doing that. "That could be complicated."

"You can also move as many people as you want, so long as they're all connected," Chloe added.

"What is your father's connection with Verde von Klaus?" Evonne asked.

"Klaus is a severely wealthy man who somehow heard about a thesis my father wrote years ago on time-travel. Before any of us knew it, my father was approached by Klaus who asked him how much it would take to make his thesis possible. Father told him and then we were shipped to a facility in Flagstaff owned by Klaus where my father lacked for nothing."

"And how did you fit into all this? You're like, what, twenty?" I asked.

"Twenty-two," she corrected me in annoyance. "I was twenty when I began helping my father in the lab."

Then she told us the rest of the story. How her father labored over a year before creating the first glove and finding out that Klaus hadn't been playing with a full deck to start with and wanted the glove for reasons that of course Chloe didn't know but were most likely evil, conniving ones. Then her father made another one in secret and hid the original bodacious one, found by yours truly, in the past.

The only hang up along the way was when Klaus found out about Dr. Atrium Spark's little swap out. "That's when Klaus took my father into custody and told me to find the other glove or he'd kill him."

"So how long have you been searching?" I inwardly grimaced when I asked.

"Over a year," she confirmed.

"Geez," I muttered. What was I supposed to say?

"So, all you need is the glove?" I asked.

Chloe brightened a little. "You'll give it back?"

"I never said that."

Deflating a little, she said, "Yes. That's all I need."

I sighed. Man, life bites sometimes. I mean, here I am,

the time-traveling billionaire who's cut short because of some crazy guy from the future with a weird name. I thought for almost a minute and came up with a plan. Not the best plan, but it had good parts for either party. "Okay, Chloe, here's the deal. Why don't we switch gloves? You tell Klaus that the other was destroyed or something, but you'll have your dad's no-kill ticket."

I could tell that Chloe wasn't too thrilled about my plan, but she could also tell that she probably wasn't going to get a better offer so she said, "Fine. I suppose you and your butler will want to get back to Chicago first?"

"Yeah, that'd be best," I said. "Grab your gear, Mitch."

Don't get me wrong, whoever-you-are, because I wasn't too thrilled about this little arrangement myself. But I was thinking that downgrading was a whole lot better than losing the glove completely.

In exactly one minute, we were all standing together in the center of the shack. Evonne put a hand on my shoulder while Chloe awkwardly placed her hand on my other shoulder.

"You kid's buckle up," I said, while punching in the date for Chicago.

I guess it wouldn't be too bad. I mean, Chloe would get her daddy back and Mitch and I would still get to be partners in time. That was the plan. Well, sort of, anyway, since apparently I wouldn't be able to take anyone with me after the downgrade.

And like most plans made when time-travel was concerned, it didn't work out.

Like, at all.

Chapter 9

"Welcome to my humble abode," I said as we appeared in my lab. "Make yourself at home. Can I get you anything?"

"Just the glove," Chloe said, glancing around. "Nice collection of weapons."

"I know, right?" I said, laughing. "Just a wee bit of blades, lass."

Chloe looked at me, extending a hand. "Seriously, the glove?"

Evonne had by this time already placed Chloe's glove in the glass case. Or I guess it was my glove now. "Okay, Chloe, I'm a man of my word."

"No, you're not."

"Okay, not really, but just this once, I am." I removed my glove, gave it a farewell pat, and then handed it over to the Russians.

Ha.

Chloe slipped it on easily, then made a face. "It's sweaty inside."

I crossed my arms. "It was either from you trying to kill me the first time, the second time, or your charming Russian personality. Take your pick."

Guess what she did. If your guess was that she glared at me, you are dead wrong, sir, or ma'am, maybe. I don't really know or care. But no, she did not glare.

Chloe smiled.

"You're insane," she said, although I noticed her smile didn't disappear. "I wouldn't care if it was left on a corpse for a year. I'm just glad I have it back."

This is a bit of an odd tale, huh? I mean, one minute Chloe's trying to kill me then the next we're laughing together and switching gloves with no problems.

Too bad it didn't remain that tranquil.

Stepping a few feet away, Chloe began punching in a date. "Thank you, Jericho. You made the right choice."

"Of course I did," I said.

Finishing the date, she hit enter, giving Evonne and me a wave. We returned the wave and waited for little Miss Russia to vanish from our lives for good.

Then she didn't vanish.

Then she didn't vanish again.

Wait. That just made, like, zero sense.

The point is she didn't go back to the future.

Geez, I really am not explaining this well, am I? Okay, start over. Chloe hit enter, waved, but then for some reason did not go forward in time.

Frowning, she glanced at the glove, punching at a few buttons on the touchscreen. After doing this for a second or two, and saying some very not-nice sounding words in Russian, she thrust her gloved hand at me in frustration, "What's wrong with this thing?"

"You had it in your possession for a grand total of literally twenty seconds, Chloe, and you've already broken it?" I scolded her while snatching the glove.

"I didn't do anything. You're the one who has had it for so long."

"Yeah, but it always worked," I muttered, examining the silver glove. "There's nothing wrong with it," I said. "Maybe it just doesn't like you."

Chloe didn't think that was very funny. "Please try not to say anything else stupid for the next two minutes."

I narrowed my eyes at her. Note: I did not glare. Distinction. She tried punching in the dates to take her home. When this attempt failed, Chloe lost it. Just how much she lost it, I cannot say, really, because I don't speak Russian and, honestly, I'm severely glad I didn't at the time since she seemed really upset about the whole glove-not-working-so-now-she-can't-save-her-father thing.

Somehow a sword ended up in her hand and I ducked before receiving its point against my neck as she backed me against the wall. "Что Вы делали к этому!" she screamed.

"I don't speak Russian!" I screamed back, holding my hands up in the air and turning my face away, eyes squeezed shut against her vehemence. "I really don't!"

"Что Вы сделали?" Chloe tried again.

I sighed, opened my eyes, and then looked at her. "You'll have to threaten me in plain old English to get what you want."

Shoulders sagging, Chloe dropped the broadsword, put her hands on her hips, looked into my eyes, and fainted.

I'm going to go with my being too shook up from her threatening my life with a broadsword to be quick enough to catch her before she hit the marble floor really hard.

Yeah. That's what I'm going to go with on this one.

And not to split hairs nor point fingers, but I didn't see Evonne jumping out like the flipping Flash and saving her from face-planting the cold floor, either. Not like he was the one about to be decapitated by a crazed Russian psycho-chick. You'd think he would've been quicker on the draw, know what I mean?

Wait. That reminds me…

"And where the Helheim were *you* when she snagged a sword and tried to kill your employer, Mitch? Taking a nap?"

Since he knew that I was, in fact, shook up, as I so wittingly put it, Evonne didn't even answer.

Yeah, that's my pal, right there. He always knows just what to say. Or just what not to say, rather. "I'm afraid madam Chloe will be needing medical attention, Master Johnson."

And, just like that, back to the butler he is.

"No way. I'm not about to have any doctors looking after little Miss Russia from the future. She's probably blood type Z, or something weird like that, anyway. Well, come on, Mitch, don't just stand there. Let's get her up to the house."

"Where shall we be taking her, sir?"

Shrugging, I picked up the crumpled girl, tossing her over my shoulder like a sack of potatoes. An extremely wonderful smelling sack of potatoes, at that. Funny how you don't notice how someone smells while fighting them for your life. "I don't know. That's you and Louise's thing. I just own the house, remember?"

"Might I suggest one of the three master bedrooms, sir? They are quite comfortable and also have all the facilities necessary to care for a patient," Evonne was saying while following me to the elevator.

Stopping suddenly before stepping inside it, I turned slightly and asked, "How bad is this, Mitch, really?"

I waited for him to answer for a few seconds. At first I thought he wasn't going to answer at all and had just started to finish my entrance inside the elevator when I heard him say, "If all the girl says is true, then I'd say this is very bad, sir," he stepped in with me and pressed a button.

"That's what I was afraid of," I said.

Chapter 10

Man, chapter ten already? I am really cranking these babies out.

Chloe ended up sleeping the rest of the night and half of the next day. She might've slept longer had Louise, my maid (but not really) and love of my life (but definitely), not shown up and begin vacuuming the hallway, thus rousing the slumbering Russian monster.

Louise is the best human ever, by the way. Definitely a lot more than just a maid. I found her from a cleaning service ad and kind of adored her. She's been with me through the first month of my coming into money and throwing wild parties, to Evonne showing up and somehow letting me know that such parties weren't cool when I housed a time-traveling device in my basement, through my need to somehow discharge a black-powder firearm at least once a day indoors, Louise was always there. I like to think of her as a cooler version of Mrs. Hudson, the old lady that took care of Sherlock Holmes and put up with all of his quite frequent shenanigans.

Chloe wasn't in a very good mood upon waking and finding herself in different clothes. My first inclination of her rising was when the elevator door opened and she burst through all fire and brimstone.

"Where are my clothes?"

"Easy there, pilgrim," I said, turning away from the flat screen I was playing Xbox on. "Next time I lose consciousness you can return the favor and put actual clean clothes on me. And don't take this the wrong way, but why're you up?"

Chloe shook her head, pinching the bridge of her nose an index finger and thumb while the other hand went to rest on her hip. I was beginning to think I'd never knew her before now. She was so uptight. Guess your father's life in the balance will take a toll on you. "Some black woman was cleaning your carpet, or something."

"Say one more word about my ebony princess and you can kiss any thought of me helping you goodbye," I told her.

Chloe must not have appreciated my comment because she just shrugged it off and aimed her crazy laser-beamed gaze at the nearest wall.

"Why aren't you working on the glove?" she asked sharply. "And what makes you think that I'm spending my precious time trying to fix your ticket home?"

Chloe just stared at me.

Shrugging, I turned back to my Xbox. "Anyway, it's not broken," I told her. "I can't pause in the middle of an online match and not get killed. Give me, oh…" I checked the kills. Yeah. My team was going to win for sure. "About six more kills. Then we'll talk about your glove."

"A most gratifying win, Master Johnson," Mitch droned behind me after my team won the match.

"Think so?" I said, powering down the screen and standing. "What's for lunch?"

"Coney Islands, sir," Mitch said. "They are awaiting you on the pavilion."

We left the lab and rode the elevator to the house, exiting and crossing the boasting room and heading toward the back yard.

The pavilion, residing on the third floor and overlooking the glorious back yard, was one of my favorite places besides the lab. Once we had seated on the slabs of solid marble benches, I swept my hand about the stone white pavilion. "Thoughts?"

Chloe hadn't said much since the basement, and following suit, she merely shrugged, her face extremely hard to read. The meal was a quiet one, to be sure. What with Chloe poking at her Coney with a fork and me eating mine like it was my last meal on earth.

"What're you thinking about?" I asked her as Evonne cleared our dishes and Louise came out with our hot tea. "I hope you like Chai tea. I'm afraid that's all I allow them to keep in stock," I told her as the love of my life placed the tray on the stone table.

"That it, kid?" Louise asked.

"That'll be all, fair maiden," I told her, extending a hand. "Go now, my dear."

Grunting, she walked off the pavilion, obviously swayed by my charm.

"So," I said, sipping at my tea. "You were about to tell me what you were thinking."

"My father," she said quietly. "And the fact that you don't seem to be the least bit worried about fulfilling your promise."

"I don't remember using the word promise, Chloe," I told her, looking over the back yard. "Plus, I was up all night thinking of a plan to get you home, and I've got to say, I believe the term easier said than done is in order here."

Evonne came out then with both of the gauntlets of time. Standing, I took both of them and sat beside Chloe. "Here's the thing, somehow it doesn't work for anyone but me," I told her, patting my glove. "Tried it on Mitch and even on Louise, which, might I add, was horrifyingly absurd of me, so don't forget all that I put at risk to help you. Neither of my employees were able to complete a successful jump, though."

Chloe stood quickly and walked to the balcony, her arms crossed tightly as she examined my backyard. Louise had put her in some clothes that an ex had left behind months ago consisting of a softball jersey and stone-washed jeans. Yes, I've had a few girlfriends that didn't last because I feel I have a problem with commitment.

What's your point?

"Look, Chloe, I know this isn't exactly going according to plan for you, but can I at least tell you my idea?"

Without turning around she lifted a shoulder. I stood and walked over to the balcony beside her with my hands in the pockets of my suit pants. I'm a bit of freak when it comes to clothes. I figured since I was rich I might as well dress like I was.

The suit I happened to be sporting that day was an Alexander Amosu and cost me a little over one-hundred grand.

"Alright, here's the deal," I started. "Since the glove isn't working for you, I will take you back home. Once we're there we'll switch gloves and part ways."

Chloe studied my face before speaking. "I know how much the glove means for someone like you. I thank you."

"Don't thank me yet," I said, turning toward the house. "Wait until you see my bill."

Chapter 11

The plan wasn't hard, really, and only had one setback, which was that even though Chloe was going to piggyback with me on the jump, her glove would still need the twelve hour recharge once we reached the other side. She gave me a quick spiel about how the process of going through time would render the glove's conductor to be blah blah blah... science science science... Russian Russian Russian... you get the idea. Geez, even in the future stuff locks up.

I'm going to skip telling you about the rest of the day, which consisted of Chloe and me preparing for our jump. Now that I think back on it, I really don't see what the big deal was. After taking away the fact that I was traveling into the future with a Russian woman to save her father's life, it was really just me giving someone a ride home from work, know what I mean?

"Where are the guns?" Chloe asked after she'd finished examining my weapon collection.

"Yeah, I don't have many of those," I told her, pointing to a back wall that Evonne opened with the stroke of a nearby keypad, revealing a few guns hanging on the backside of it. "Also, why would we need any?"

"It's a long story," Chloe muttered, her back to me while she selected a few handguns.

I really don't like guns. I'm not scared of them and they have their place, but give me the good old days where civilized men killed each other with sharpened pieces of metal or their fists any day.

"My favorite," I said, snapping my fingers. "Evonne, have us some sushi tacos flown in from LA, please. We'll be a while."

Chloe slammed a pistol she'd been holding back onto the rack. "We won't be a while. Do you not realize that there might actually be some things that you do not have to know?"

I held up my hands and was about to tell her to chill and that I didn't have to know but she wasn't finished.

"Everyone fights where I'm from, Jericho. I'm twenty-two years old and there has never been one year of peace, plenty, or relaxation. Flagstaff isn't a pretty city filled with malls or restaurants anymore. It's a warzone, one of the only surviving cities left on the entire planet and everyone wants a piece. The streets are crawling with Фашисты by day and the играющие на понижение by night."

"I don't speak Russian," I said for the hundredth time.

"The Fascists by day and the Bears by night," she corrected herself before frowning and looking at me like I'd just appeared. "Since you won't be staying long, I don't suppose it's necessary to have your brain imprinted."

Wait. What?

"So let's go, then," Chloe said, strapping on the holsters of a few handguns she thought worthy enough to bring with us. "You do know how to use one of these things if the situation arises, right?"

"Of course I do. It's just that—"

"Just what? That you thought this would be another field trip and learning experience?" she shot at me.

"Yeah, kind of," I confessed, grabbing a Berretta, a sub-machine gun and some ammo. "I mean, it's been a while since I've used a gun, but I think my rusty skills coupled with a little adrenaline and a dash of not-really-wanting-to-die will be enough to last me twelve hours."

"Let's hope so," Chloe said, crossing to the center of the lab. I finished strapping on my guns before following her. She'd by this time changed back into her now clean black jumpsuit and I foolishly was about to go to the future in my favorite expensive suit and black Chuck Taylor's.

"Evonne, it is now 7:30. I'll be back at 8:00 expecting my sushi tacos."

"It will be done, Master Johnson," my butler replied. "Be

careful, sir."

I could tell Evonne wasn't really digging the whole Russian-occupied-America-future-jump thing but I could also tell he knew I'd be back at 8:00 one way or another.

I, too, thought that I'd be munching on sushi tacos at exactly 8:03, telling my relieved butler of my many futuristic adventures while sporting my downgraded gauntlet of time.

But, as I've been telling you, whoever-you-are, making plans as far as time-travel is concerned is just about as mental as you can get. If you don't understand, please listen the next two minutes.

Chloe gave me the coordinates and the exact date while grabbing my shoulder. I punched in the numbers she was feeding me then took a deep breath, "Ready?"

"I was about to ask you that," Chloe said, her hand tightening on my shoulder. "This will land us well outside the city near a safe house I know of. We'll exchange gloves and you'll wait your twelve hours inside of the safe house while I sneak back into Flagstaff."

Well, it seemed I wouldn't be experiencing the battle-riddled streets of 2340 Flagstaff, Arizona after all. Shrugging, I hit enter. "It's your future, Chloe. I'm just along for the ride."

Then we started fading out of 2012 and into 2340.

Oh well. I guess it was for the best that I wasn't going to come in contact with any locals. I mean, sure I wanted to check out some sights, but I suppose my whole role here was to help Chloe and not satisfy my desire for knowledge.

Then we were standing in the whitest sand you've ever seen. Wait. Not sand.

"Snow?" I growled, wrapping my arms around myself as the white flurries whirled around us. "Are you kidding me, Chloe? You couldn't have suggested a, oh, I don't know, coat, maybe? Or a thermos of
hot chocolate..."

I never finished my sarcastic rant because something smallish, roundish, and grenadeish landed at my feet.

Seriously? I had been there for a grand total of ten seconds and already had a flipping grenade blinking at my feet?

We interrupt Jericho Johnson's inevitable demise to bring you this public service announcement:

To all my single bros out there: Bad things happen to guys that are too nice. It's true. We try and help people, okay, mostly female people, because we're just naturally nice guys. But then there comes a time when your niceness is abused and you're dragged three-hundred years into the future, where it's freezing, might I add, and what do you get out of all the nice and helpful things you've been doing? A trophy? Nope. A medal? Wrong. A lollipop? Not even close.

You get a grenade at your feet.

Whew. Glad that's off my chest. I feel tons better after letting you all know that, seriously. You're a great listener, whoever-you-are.

Now, where the Helheim was I before the public service announcement?

Oh, right, the grenade at my feet.

Not much to tell, really, because it seemed that the grenades in 2340 stared at by an idiot not two feet away did the exact same thing that the old fashioned 2012 grenades did when stared at by an idiot not two feet away.

They go boom. Yep, just like the old ones.

Chapter 12

The explosion was accompanied by a bright blue flash and then I was flying through the air. Not in a cool, Superman fashion, either. It was more of a pinwheel/barrel-roll/oh-my-gosh-that-hurt-so-bad kind of flying through the air.

I landed on my back and slid about fifteen foot before hitting something hard. Groaning, I felt it with my hand. I'd hit something concrete.

All thoughts of the flash grenade forgotten, no it wasn't a blow-your-legs-off kind of grenade, I rolled onto my stomach and tried to get to my feet, which was accomplished with the aid of the wall in front of me.

"Chloe?" I called.

Then a red dot appeared on the back of my left hand, which was resting on the wall. A man somewhere in the whiteness of snow shouted in Russian, and in seconds more red dots appeared, only these were crawling all over my body like insects.

The next belt of Russian I heard sounded harsh and like it was addressing me. Not knowing what else to do, I held up both my hands, placing them behind my head. When my fingers laced together, I felt the cold of my glove and remembered why I was there in the first place.

Where the heck was Chloe, anyway? Had I alone survived the flash grenade and her corpse was freezing in the snow somewhere I couldn't see?

I didn't have time to dwell on this long because my attackers materialized from the white blusters of wind in front of me. Man, the visibility was literally about twenty feet. Also something that Chloe could've mentioned before she had me out here freezing away in my $186,000 suit, but since she also could have been dead at the time, I shook the thought from my mind.

There were seven of them total and, dude, but were they wild looking. I'm going to attempt to describe a few of these hellions for you.

The first thing that jumped out at me were the helmets, wicked looking things with smoky eyes that glowed florescent red with a hose coming from each side of the mouthpiece and running behind their shoulders, attaching to something I couldn't see. They all wore body armor which also had sections of it that glowed the same florescent red of the eyes. Veins of the light pulsed up and down the muscular looking arms and legs and all met at the center of the chest piece, which illuminated a symbol in yellow.

Uh oh. I recognized the symbol instantly.

It was a hammer and a sickle crossing.

This day was turning out to be a bad one. The seven demonic looking men were now standing in front of me which gave me a chance to get a good look at their hardware. The guns they were all sporting were like nothing I'd ever seen before and, just as I had hoped deep down inside, they looked freakishly from the future.

"Государство ваше название, гражданское лицо," one of them told me, his voice laden with static from the mask.

"I don't speak Russian," I told him, shrugging my shoulders while keeping my fingers laced behind my head.

I don't know if you've ever had the chance to speak with a Russian Darth Vader, so let me tell you, they're hard to read. Not seeing the face was one reason behind it and the language barrier wasn't helping matters.

"Английский язык?" I heard another ask.

The man who'd addressed me first was the only one of the soldiers who never took his glowing red eyes off me while the other six glanced at each other and exchanged Russian questions and answers to one another. I could tell they were puzzled by something. Well, at least the six jabber-mouths were, to be sure. The man who'd decided that a staring match was in order wasn't partaking of the confused talk, and I was starting to feel more nervous about my little predicament.

Then Mr. Stare held up a clenched fist, silencing his chattering platoon. He took a step toward me and I involuntarily took a step back, or would have had I not been up against a concrete wall.

Mr. Stare was close to me now. The smell that emanated from the suit was a mixture of a little motor oil, fried motherboard, and a hint of gun powder. He stared at me and I returned the menacing stare right back. Although, now that I think about it, I'm pretty sure he wasn't feeling the least bit threatened by me.

What can I say? I gave it my best shot, I guess.

His right hand reached for his helmet and I could hear gears gyrating and whining as he did so. It was actually so futuristically nerdy that I got chills when I heard it and instantly knew that if I didn't get killed by this dude, I was definitely going to ask him where I could pick up a suit of my own before heading home.

Mr. Stare tapped a button somewhere on the right side of his helmet, and with a resounding hiss and a little cloud of steam, the face part rose from the chin and I got my first real look at his face. When I realized what was happening, I had a few last second thoughts of what I wanted this soldier from 2340's face to look like.

And I was not disappointed.

The first thing I noticed was that his left eye was gone and had been replaced with what my fan boy mind could only discern as a cyborg one, which glowed yellow. The right eye seemed to be normal but there were several dark rings around both sockets, indicating that he probably spent more time wearing his mask than not.

His skin was ghostly white and his features, which were hard to notice because he seemed to not have eyebrows, were blank.

Reaching toward me with an armored hand pulsating with red glow, he grabbed my chin, the cold metallic fingers squeezing my cheeks together and causing me to draw back quickly and bang my head against the stupid wall.

"Английский язык?"

"Look, I said I don't speak Russian," I said in agitation, "English, okay?"

For those of you who were around at the beginning of my story, you might be thinking of saying, "But Jericho, doesn't your glove decipher languages for you?"

I really hope you guys remember that because right then, in the snowy hills of 2340 surrounded by ferocious hell troopers making demands in another language, I, your adorable story-telling amigo, Jericho Johnson, did not.

Apparently Mr. Stare wasn't too thrilled about my getting short-fused with him, if the slamming of his mask and shouting of orders at his men was anything to go by. The seven of them stalked away from me about fifteen feet and turned around, cocking their rifles.

Death by firing squad seemed to be the only thing on my menu right then, and let me tell you, it wasn't looking appetizing in the least. "Hey, come on, guys," I said quickly, my pulse going overtime while I held my hands up higher in the air. "We're all warm-blooded mammals with opposable thumbs here, right? Why all the hostility?"

Then a female Russian voice came from behind them and they all turned away from me.

Yes. Chloe to the rescue.

Except that just when I thought little Miss Russia had finally come to save me, the platoon parted a little and I got a look at what I thought was Chloe.

My shoulders sagged when I saw it was just another one of the red troopers. The seven men started speaking to her. I guess it was a woman, I mean, it sounded like one, anyway, but the cyborg suits weren't exactly the most flattering as far as a woman's figure was concerned.

They pointed to me, explaining the situation of the freezing billionaire that they were about to use as target practice. Nodding, the newcomer stepped into line and leveled her rifle at me.

Wow. I know I've already told you guys how much the day was starting to stink but, man, a firing squad? Really? In the snow?

Geez.

I closed my eyes and turned my face away. "I can't believe my sushi tacos are going to go to waste."

Those were my last words before I heard the first gun fire.

Chapter 13

My lucky number thirteen.

The discharged rifle that made me wince and scream like a five-year-old getting a flu shot didn't send flames of pain through my body nor send explosions of concrete whirling around me. The gun kept firing and I glanced at my attackers who were being attacked by the eighth trooper.

I say attacked, but since they were all focusing on me and all she really did was take two quick steps to the right and spray a hailstorm of bullets into the men lined up like ducklings, it was really murder.

But do you think I cared about what correct wording my salvation needed right then? I most certainly did not.

The female trooper ran to me and opened her mask.

"You certainly have a way with people," Chloe said, her face illuminated in red glow.

"My devilishly good looks that all the ladies love sometimes make men want to put me against a wall and shoot me to death," I told her, lowering my arms which had fallen asleep somewhere through my bout with the Russian monsters. "Nice suit."

Chloe shrugged, and I again heard the clicking and gyrating of gears and small pistons as she lifted a shoulder. I had to fight the urge not to kiss her again. Curse you, inner nerd, curse you to Helheim and back.

"What were those guys?" I asked, wrapping my arms around myself for warmth as I made my way to what was left of the seven troopers. "Ah," I muttered in disgust, "I see you hit them all in the head."

"Lucky for us," Chloe said coming to a stop beside me as I squatted down and poked a finger at a dead man's chest plate. "The side of the helmet is the only vulnerable spot on the S-16.

Just be glad it wasn't an S-20. Then it would have been *our* corpses being prodded right now."

The red glow that ran through the veins of the suits had faded into blackness within seconds of the occupant's death. "I'm guessing the S-20 is a lot bigger?"

"The biggest yet but it still has its weaknesses."

Standing, I took my first look at my surroundings. The safe house seemed to be on some sort of hill, but I couldn't be sure because of the lack of visible distance.

Then I remembered that I was freezing to death. "Say, Chloe, where does a guy get warm clothes in 2340?"

Chloe smiled and tapped an ironclad boot against one of the soldiers she'd just wasted. "Let's find your size, shall we?"

Instantly I squatted back down to begin my selection. "Best day ever."

The inside of the safe house was about as normal as a safe house in the future could be if Chloe's nonchalance was anything to go by. But to me it was like the fan-flipping-tastic Starship Enterprise.

I already felt amazing strutting around in my new S-16 suit, bending and moving my arms and legs just to hear the awesome sounds the suit made. Chloe had sat down at a desk and was tapping away at a flat projection that floated above it whilst I was getting used to my new duds.

She had given me a rundown on what the S-16 was capable of while she helped me get into one, and my smile and eyes grew larger with each word she spoke. I grabbed a random desk and lifted it with one arm. Laughing, I put the desk back down and leaped into the air, touching the drafty ceiling nearly fifteen feet high.

"This is the greatest day of my life!" I shouted at the top of my lungs, cutting a perfect no-handed back flip and landing easily. "How fast did you say I can run in this thing?"

Chloe, who'd no doubt been in one of the suits since she was three, didn't look away from the screen she was frowning at when she answered. "About sixty miles per hour."

"BRB," I told her before darting outside into the snow.

"Wait, Jericho—" but I was gone.

I hit the snow-covered ground running and within seconds I was bounding at what I was guessing was top speed because I couldn't go any faster. The frigid wind felt wonderful on my face. All the masks were too mutilated for me to wear. I skidded to a halt close to an outcropping of bare trees, touched one, then I was bolting back to the safe house as fast as my suit's legs would carry me.

Chloe was still tapping at the flat screen and frowning when I ducked back inside, not even breathing hard. "Have fun?"

"You have no idea," I said, sitting on a nearby stool then screaming as it crumbled beneath me and I landed on my back.

Chloe still didn't take her eyes off the screen as she tapped her metal-knuckled hand on the stone bench that I just noticed was her desk chair. "The S-16s weigh nearly four-hundred pounds and aren't currently used in actual battle anymore due to EMP bursts."

"What?" I said, rolling over and getting to my feet. "Are you kidding me? If they had, like, ten of these back in 2001, the Iraqi campaign would've literally lasted twelve hours."

Chloe stopped tapping at the screen and turned her head slightly in my direction. "How old do you think that suit you're wearing is?"

I frowned, not expecting that, and gave my suit a glance over. Chloe had left the right forearm piece off of my suit so I could still use my glove with no problems. Opening and closing my hands as I stared at them, I said, "I don't know. Got some wear on it, I guess, so maybe ten years?"

Chloe's burst of laughter made me jump it was so sudden.

"Okay," I said, seeing that I was wrong. "Twenty years?"

"Try almost two-hundred," Chloe said, getting the reins on her funny horse. "What part of currently not used in actual combat did you not understand?"

"Oh?" I shot at her. "And I suppose that the seven guys you just hosed right outside weren't in combat at all. Maybe they were just taking a leisure stroll wearing armor and toting assault rifles."

Chloe had once again returned to tapping away at the screen. "Those were just a few rogue fascists with neither motive nor brains. Perfectly feral at best."

"Enlighten me, dearest Chloe, about which side you are on in this case. You mentioned the Fascists and the Lions."

"Bears."

"Lions, tigers, bears—whatever," I said. "Anyway, which side are you on?"

"Neither," she replied simply.

"So that makes you what?"

"Фракция."

"Oh, my flipping gosh, I don't speak Russian," I said, annoyed. "You speak perfect English with a hot Russian accent to go with it."

Chloe stood suddenly. "Возьмите место, пожалуйста," she told me, waving at the bench she'd been occupying.

Frowning, I crossed the room and sat down.

"Смотрите на экран, Иерихон," she said, pointing at the screen.

Sighing, because it seemed I'd lost the language war, I peered at the screen. "Great," I said, scowling. "Even the crap you're making me look at is in Russian. Great job, Chloe."

Chloe wasn't listening because she had started tapping again at the screen with one hand while reaching into a drawer with the other. She finished tapping at the green hologram and produced what looked like a headset from the drawer she'd been rummaging in.

Chloe then got behind me and started placing the headset on me, all the while jabbering in Russian. "Это - сканер нейрона. Это не использовалось в в то время как,потому что только нет очень многих американцев,оставленных , чтобы нуждаться в том."

Nodding just because I thought it would make her shut up, I tried not to sigh while she placed cold metal pads to my temples. Then I felt her hands on my suit shoulders. "Готовый?"

Since I figured she'd just asked me if I was ready, I nodded again. "Sure," I said sarcastically. "Please have a defibrillator on hand just in case I happen to die of excitement."

Chloe reached over my shoulder and tapped once somewhere on the screen.

I felt a small vibration coming from the pads attached to my temples, but it wasn't anything unbearable. Then things started projecting in front of me. It was just one symbol at a time that floated for about five seconds each before being replaced by yet another five second symbol. I was guessing that what she wanted me to do was just stare at the meaningless symbols like I actually cared, so that's what I did.

The boring tutorial of whatever only lasted around two minutes, so I didn't have to watch very long. Which was cool because for some reason watching the symbols fade in and out was starting to give me a small headache. "Are we done now?" I asked, rubbing at my left eye.

"Нет, еще," she said in Russian.

But guess what I heard her say?

"No, not yet."

Before I could say anything, Chloe tapped the screen again somewhere.

"Вы только что успешно закончили нервный просмотр русского языка.Спасибо за участие ." Is what projected in front of me.

And guess what it said?

"You have just successfully finished the neural scan of the Russian language. Thank you for participating," I read aloud.

"Браво, Иерихон," Chloe said, smiling and clapping her hands together, the resounded clangs of metal ringing around the room. "Bravo, Jericho."

I stood. This was incredible. Bowing low, I said, "Twas ничто, действительно.Как я мог взять кредит на чью-либо умную разработку?" which translated to, "Twas nothing, really. How could I take credit for someone else's clever engineering?"

So, yeah, now I was fluent in Russian.

And before moving on to chapter fourteen, let me address the question bouncing around your right-frontal lobe, which is, "Did you learn any other languages while you were there, Jericho?"

So, just for you, I'll answer your question so you can have some closure.

噢,但我沒有。 蓬勃發展。 完全是不願意為中國的,是你嗎?

Chapter 14

"So, what's the plan?" I asked Chloe, scooting over on the stone bench so she could sit beside me.

"Nothing, really," she said, accepting the seat. "I've been going through the attack reports over the past month trying to decide which route I should take entering the city. I figured you running around in an S-16 for a few minutes wouldn't hurt anything."

Smiling, I went to take off my glove. "You're the best, Chloe."

Then something horrifying caught my eye.

The screen on my glove was black. Something I'd never seen before. Not being like a laptop or anything, in a *lot* more ways than one, meant that I had never actually powered the thing down before. I mean, why would I? It never did anything but glow and look awesome since I unearthed it on my hiking trip of destiny. Thoughts like batteries or charging, in my defense, were lost to whoever looked at the glove, really, because it just appeared as futuristic as it was.

But I didn't know everything about it, so maybe my battery had finally gone out.

Which wasn't a bad thought, really, because I suppose that if it had to run out of juice, running out just before I swapped it for another one was about as good of timing as I could think of.

"Say, Chloe?"

"Yeah?"

"I hope you got some D batteries for this thing, because I'm thinking my Coppertops have finally run their course," I said, extending my glove to her.

She glanced at it, gasped, grabbed it, and said in a low cold voice, "Why is the screen off?"

Frowning and furrowing my brow a little, I stated that

it was her dad's gizmo that she'd helped create so maybe she should have asked herself that question.

Chloe had removed the glove by this time and was freaking big time, man. Jabbing at the screen, Chloe started spouting Russian, which was kind of her thing, you know, when she got really mad or upset. Only this time I was able to understand everything she was angrily muttering and I was one-hundred percent correct on my first analogy of this being some not-so-nice things she had been saying before.

After not getting any results with her finger jabbing, Chloe raised the dead glove above her head and would have slammed it on the stone table had I not snatched it out of her hands first.

"Easy, Chloe. Chill out, man."

"No," she screamed, darting her fingers to her glove. Her screen was on, but barely and flickering out quickly.

Then it was all quiet except for Chloe's ragged breathing. I looked at my dead glove. "Any ideas?"

"The EMP grenade."

Oh. And I'd thought it was just your average flash-bang grenade. Man, I really needed to get with the times.

"My father warned me about heavy electric fields. He told me not to get too close." Chloe was on the verge of something. Not tears, exactly, so I'm not sure what she was on the verge of. "He said that too much electrical current was one of the only things that could penetrate the scandium casing."

"So I'm thinking that a whole grenade of the stuff wasn't good for my baby."

"Neither of our babies," Chloe corrected, standing.

"Whoa," I told her with my hands held up. "We've known each other for way too short of a time to be discussing children already."

"My father is the only one that can fix them," Chloe said, either not hearing the joke meant to lighten the mood or choosing to ignore it.

I don't know where my mind had been the past two

minutes, but apparently it was gone to some faraway land because the gravity of the situation finally hit home. "Your father?"

Chloe, who I was guessing just caught on to the apparent fix, too, looked at me and simply nodded.

"The same father being held by some crazy guy with an army of gun-wielding sociopaths?"

Again, Chloe just nodded, looking at me the way a soccer mom looks at her kid when she has to tell him that he won't be getting that ice-cream stop he'd been expecting.

Not knowing what else to do, I sat back down.

Let me interject here that I am a strong-willed kind of guy. I mean, it takes a lot to shake my focus and not a whole lot shocks me. Time-travel will do that to a guy.

But since it wasn't, in fact, time-travel but the lack thereof that I was presented with, things were starting to look bleak.

"I can still get into the city, Jericho, but you're now presented with two options."

"And those are?" asked the dejected hero of this sad yet true tale.

"These shelters have blast doors that seal from the inside and aren't easily damaged. You could wait here while I free my father and fix the gloves and I'll be back as soon as I can."

"So the blast door will hold off whoever happens upon the shelter that's normally open to the public, and the fact that its sealed shut won't make them want to crack it open?" I asked the reasonable question.

Chloe shrugged.

"That's what I thought. And behind door number two?"

"You come with me," she said simply. "It will be dangerous, but you can leave as soon as the gloves are fixed."

I shook my head, standing. "Your dad isn't chilling in his lab in the backyard. He's on lock down by the guy you have to bring the glove to. Something tells me he's not going to like getting his prize back broken."

"It can't be helped. I'll tell him it was damaged in the

retrieval and that my father can fix it if it comes to that," Chloe told me, walking to one of the chrome cabinets across the room. When she opened it, I saw that it contained more guns. "I'm not planning on coming in the front door, anyway."

"Do you people ever have anything other than deadly weapons behind closed doors?"

"Most of the time, no," she said as she pulled out a few of the bodacious assault rifles I'd seen the demon troopers packing. "You'll see why in a minute."

I caught the rifle she'd tossed to me and turned it over a few times. "I'm guessing it works like the guns back home? Like, point it at baddies and squeeze the trigger?"

Chloe walked back to me and gave me the rundown on my new piece, showing me how to turn the laser sight on and off, how to reload, and how to switch to the frag launcher. I nodded throughout the lecture on ballistics, watching her.

"What?" she asked after she'd finished and noticed me staring at her.

"You're very attractive when you spout all your gun knowledge."

I wasn't ready for the punch she delivered to my shoulder in what I was hoping was the same way most girls punched guys in the shoulder. You know like the whole giggly, "Oh, stop it, you handsome man, you."

But since we were both rocking the S-16s, Chloe's playful punch was heard more than felt and the sharp steel-on-steel sound resounded around the room after she delivered it.

"Good," I said, cocking the assault rifle. "Glad to see that I'm not the only one who's hitting on someone around here."

Chapter 15

What.

Chapter fifteen already? Geez.

As thrilled as I am about how fast and amazing this little memoir is going, I have to say that fifteen was, like, the absolute worst age of my life.

I mean, it was my first year of college, when I was made fun of for being the youngest guy in the room and other uncomfortable stuff like that.

Anyway, I figure since I hate fifteen so much, and since it is my memoir, after all, I'm just going to skip this chapter. That good with everyone?

Cool. Moving on.

Chapter 16

"What're you doing?" I shouted at Chloe as she jumped over me, bolting as fast as her suit would carry her toward the behemoth of machinery that occupied the center of the street, still spraying bullets everywhere with the two massive guns attached to its forearms.

Scrambling to my shaky feet, I monkey-crawled deeper into the alleyway, screaming like a lunatic while concrete exploded all around me. Once deeper I figured I'd take a break and revise the situation, but apparently the S-20 had other plans for me as the walls around me started getting hit, too. "Un-flipping-believable," I grumbled, getting to my feet and dashing down the snow-ridden alley. Although the suit was amazing, I was still breathing hard and my heart was beating like the bass drum at a death metal concert.

Leaping to my left, I kicked off the brick wall and shot to the opposite wall, which I ran up like a ninja, the heavy feet of the suit digging deep into the wall with each step. When I reached the top I kicked off again, landing on the other building before bolting to the edge almost fifty feet away, skidding to a stop and peering down at the battle.

Chloe was kneeling in front of the mech, her hands behind her head as the twenty-foot machine from hell took the last step, stopping in front of her.

Wow. That was fast. And here I thought she was the one who was saving the day.

Oh, well.

No one lives forever, they tell me.

Wait.

Okay, I get it now. You guys are totally lost because I skipped chapter fifteen, aren't you? Alright, fine, I'll go back and tell you fifteen but only because I can't stand gaps.

Remember that. This is for me, not you.
I don't even know you.

Chapter 15
(Continued)

We exited the bunker and I was reminded yet again that my suit was lacking a helmet. Chloe donning hers was one reminder but the frigid wind slicing into my face was the biggest one.

Instinctively I checked my glove to see how cold it was and grimaced. The black screen was the worst reminder yet.

We made one last stop at the bodies Chloe had chalked up, to make sure that at least one helmet was usable and, as luck would have it, one turned out to be.

"Got this one in the neck," Chloe said with about as much ease as a golfer would mention a birdie. I caught it when she tossed it to me. Then I noticed the blood all over it and made a face.

"Gross," was all I said before sliding it over my head. It wasn't too gross, though, because the blood was frozen.

Yeah, *that* made wearing a blood-covered helmet not as gross, right?

"Don't be such a baby," I heard Chloe's voice crackle in my ear.

"Just next time maybe a little less frozen blood?" I shot over to her.

"Tell me, Jericho," Chloe began, taking a step away from me. I noticed her right foot was slowly twisting slightly on the snow-covered ground, the universal sign for catch-me-if-you-can. "Do you like your woman fast, or is that just a fabricated exterior?"

I opened my mouth to tell her that I simply adored fast women, but I never got the chance to say it because she bolted into the mist, kicking up snow as she did so.

"Oh, no, she didn't," I muttered before speeding after her. She must not really have been trying to get away from me because when the cap speed was close to sixty miles an hour, whoever got the head start wasn't about to get caught. So when I loped up beside her I said, "Hi. Beautiful day, ain't it?"

This was meant to be sarcastic due to the extremely unbeautiful day we were running through at that moment, so I was kind of thrown when she said, "Yes, very."

After running at top speed for almost five minutes, we both skidded to a halt on what appeared to be a large white embankment that overlooked what I was guessing was Flagstaff.

Or what was left of it.

The city looked like a snapshot from any zombie apocalypse film you could think of. Large buildings here and there missing huge sections of important structural spots on them and no lights on anywhere. The only signs of life were the large smokestacks that seemed to border the entire city, billowing black smog like crazy.

"I'm guessing you guys aren't exactly green folks around here," I said.

When Chloe asked what the heck I was talking about, I went on to explain about all the save-the-earth jazz that was going on back home, which led me to a thought.

"Did the icecaps ever melt?" I asked, turning away from Flagstaff to look at her.

"The what?"

"You know, the polar icecaps. Did they melt?"

Chloe wasn't exactly sure what I was asking, but she figured if I was thinking of a landmark or standing structure, that I could pretty much bet on it being nonexistent after World War III.

"Wait, hold up," I said, perplexed. "I remember you saying something about a World War IV back at the lab. Three wasn't bad enough to mention?"

"Normally we don't count the third World War because it was less than ten minutes long," Chloe said, shrugging.

"Wow. Did, uh, America or Russia fire first?"

"Russia. But not on America. We hit South Africa and Finland."

"Why? Nukes are the norm in 2012, don't get me wrong, but what changed that made people, I don't know, actually use them?"

"The rest of the world all believe it was because we were the next target. We had been at war for over a decade with Finland, and South Africa had just joined the Finnish against us."

I frowned. "You say rest of the world like that's not the real reason you guys fired."

"Because it's not the real reason," she said, hitting a button and lifting her mask. I took this as a cue and lifted my mask. "We all thought that when the time finally came, mother Russia would win with honor," she took a few steps closer to me, which was fine with me except that all flirtatiousness was out of the question due to the way she looked as she talked.

"In the end all it took was for someone high on the ladder to have too much vodka. Thus the start and end of World War III."

"You mean this is all that's left of the world because some schmuck's vodka bottle happened to be sitting right next to a Defcon 1 button?" I asked, sweeping my left hand toward Flagstaff.

Chloe turned away as her mask clamped down. "Welcome to the future, Jericho."

I fell in step behind her as we made our way down the slope toward Flagstaff. "But you guys have the gloves," I told her. "You could have zipped back and stopped Otis Campbell from nuking the planet."

"Can't," she said simply. "Can we drop it?"

Chloe was irritated, that much was certain. I'm guessing it was mostly due to Russia's premature nuke fest, which I was also guessing was embarrassing to any Russian, but I could tell that I'd struck a chord with my time-travel idea.

"Why?"

"I said drop it," she growled.

Grabbing her shoulder, I whirled her around to face me. "Tell me why, Chloe." I wasn't trying to be irritating but her irritation was irritating me.

I couldn't see her face because of her helmet, but I could feel the glare. "And what would knowing the answer do for you, Jericho?"

I let go of her shoulder. "Just tell me."

Although I could see she wasn't too thrilled about it, Chloe said, "Fallout."

"Yeah, I noticed," I said, looking around. "Don't tell me that's the reason."

"Generally, yes," she said. "After the warheads went off everything changed. Not only did it move the planet further from the sun, thus beginning the everlasting ice age, but it also messed up earth's core structure, as well. Or fixed it, as my father would say."

"Maybe fixed it if you were a mammoth," I muttered, glancing around at the snowy landscape.

"Or trying to create a time-traveling device," Chloe said. "After the restructure, which was one of the real reasons most cities collapsed, new elements were discovered, one of which resides in all three gloves."

Taking all of this in wasn't the easiest thing in the world. Just saying. But I was pretty sure I knew the reason now.

"So, you're saying that since the gloves were only created because of nuclear fallout, then any notion of using the fallout offspring to go back and stop fallout from happening is out of the question?"

Chloe turned around and resumed her trudge with me close behind. "Brilliant," was all she said, still ticked that I'd made her explain the whole drunk-Russian-nuke story.

The rest of the journey to the edge of Flagstaff was silent. Chloe was probably just fuming, although I wasn't so sure about her thoughts.

Entering the city was a cinch. I thought it was going to include ninja-like reflexes and maximum stealth—wait, that's an oxymoron because ninja-like reflexes states that maximum stealth has already been initiated—anyway, the point is that entering the city turned out to be simple. One minute we were walking toward Flagstaff, the next we were walking in it.

I mean, don't get me wrong, I love it when I can walk without dodging bullets, but I was at least expecting a few unmanned turrets or something equally as sentinel-like, you know?

Abandoned cars lined the streets, their broken-out windows and flat tires looking ever so…

Wait.

There weren't any tires on the scrapped cars.

Where were the tires, you might ask? Okay, you might not so I'll just say welcome to the future, Will Robinson.

I've only been to the 2012 Flagstaff once in my lifetime and although the air was a little thin for my taste, the journey did end with my coming home with a time-traveling glove so I guess I can't really judge the city too much. After living in Chicago, the streets of Flagstaff had felt severely spread out to me and all drivers had plenty of room to get around without killing someone.

Future Flagstaff didn't even look sort of like the one I remembered and not because of the whole nuclear wasteland feel, either. The entire city structure was different now, complete with thin streets, tall cramped buildings on both sides, and lots of messed up future cars.

"You sure we're not in New York?" I asked Chloe, glancing around.

"Get down," was her reply, her voice low in my ear.

Not knowing what else to do, I ducked into an alley and behind a dumpster, squatting low and putting my back against the brick wall. Then I noticed that Chloe was right beside me.

"Hey, good-looking," I said, smiling behind my helmet.

"Shut up, fool," she whispered. "There's an S-20 in the streets."

That shut me up. I mean, one minute we were skipping through the streets all cake and ice-cream then the next we were ducking for cover. The concrete shook beneath me as whatever we were hiding from stomped down the streets, each step resounding loudly in the alley.

Dropping my voice to a whisper, I asked in my quietest voice just how big an S-20 was, exactly, because it felt like Godzilla was coming.

"It can't hear us but keep your voice down, anyway," Chloe said, and then I saw the shadow. The S-20 had stopped right in front of the alley where we were hiding like rats, and although I couldn't see it because of the dumpster, the tall silhouette that was cast along the damp snow-covered alleyway was very discernible.

Gulping as I peered at the enormous shadow cast by the S-20, I asked in a whisper, "Is that an Autobot or a Decepticon? Because I'm on whichever side this guy's on."

Then a lot of stuff happened at once. The first of which was that the dumpster we were hiding behind was ripped from the pavement with ease by the S-20. It didn't look anything like any Transformer I'd ever seen before, by the way.

And it was a lot less friendly.

"Ah!" I screamed, scrambling backward when the huge mech turned two Gatling guns our way and started firing.

"Hide, Jericho," Chloe shouted, leaping over me and running toward the—

Wait. We finally caught up with where I started. Whew. Finally. See? And you thought you were missing out on some big, huge, crazy part of the story, didn't you?

I tried to skip it but you said no.

And don't even try to pin finishing chapter 15 on me. That was all you, whoever-you-are.

Just saying.

Chapter 16
(Continued)

I pulled my assault rifle around, switching it to frag mode and leveling down. "Alright, Jericho. You wanted adventure? This is about as adventuresome as you're going to get, buddy."

Aiming at the crumbling street right behind the S-20, because, you know, Chloe happened to be right in front of it and that seemed the best place at the time, I took a deep breath before launching my first grenade.

Concrete flew in all directions as the frag exploded on impact, causing the mammoth S-20 to rock on is mammoth legs a bit, which was all Chloe needed.

In a split second she was soaring into the air, cutting a double front flip before landing on top of the mech's dome head. Well, it wasn't really a head, per say. The body of S-20 was made to resemble a human figure, all but where there should have been a head there was a dome-like area where the pilot sat, peering out at the world through the God-knows-how-thick ballistic glass, the touchscreen buttons, switches, and gadgets on the said glass visible and backwards for anyone who found themselves unfortunate enough to see the pilot fingering out commands of death on the tinted dome.

Unless it happened to be Chloe Sparks, someone who happened to know the S-20's sweet spot.

Drawing back a curled steel-clad fist, Chloe delivered the blow of all blows directly in the center of the dome before crawling quickly to the rocking S-20's top and leaping on the other side, crossing her arms over her chest and slipping through the hole my frag had created in the street and disappearing below.

The pilot had by this time regained some of the S-20's composure and started looking around for his two missing targets.

I frowned. Shouldn't Chloe's amazing fist bump of doom, I don't know, have broken the glass shield or at least have cracked it? I'm not a picky person most of the time so I would've been thrilled with at least a scratch, or something.

Then it happened.

The dome started cracking from the center, spreading out slowly at first before the veins picked up speed and the entire dome was one big shatter.

I'm going to take a shot in the dark here and say that I'm pretty sure that the dude in the pilot seat couldn't see a dang thing. Partly because it looked that way and partly because the panicking pilot began spinning the S-20 in a complete 360, swiveling it at the waist while firing wildly with his humongous Gatling guns.

Let's not forget that Chloe was baby-blanket safe under the street while I, who was not, had to leap thirty feet backward to avoid being cut in half by bullets as they made their way to my rooftop due to the crazy carousel of death.

"Jericho," Chloe's voice buzzed in my helmet.

"Yes, dearest?" I cooed, darting quickly to my right to avoid more of the bullets that cut through the building beneath me like butter. My only inclinations of the approaching waves of hot lead were the visible slices that sped toward me. "Can he see?"

"No," Chloe confirmed. "But he knows that we won't attack while he's firing like a maniac."

"So what's the plan, Stan?" I asked, again having to dart out of the way of yet more bullets. "And, please, take your time. I actually enjoy being buffeted by near-death experience after near-death experience so joke's on you."

"The glass dome is weakened. All it needs is one of your grenades," Chloe said. "Can you get close enough?"

"If I wanted to die, yes, I'd say getting close enough to pop off a grenade or two wouldn't be hard. But news flash," I rolled out of the way of another bullet wave, "I don't."

"Listen to me, Jericho," Chloe screamed, her lecture cut short as I heard a huge groaning sound. "It's coming through the street. Do it now."

Without thinking I sprinted to the end of the building. "Get away from it," I shouted, performing the best swan dive imaginable off the side of the twelve-story building. Or it would have been a swan dive had my arms been spread out in serenity instead of wielding an assault rifle, which I brandished in mid-dive, soaring directly over the S-20.

I literally felt bullets cut through the air all around me as I aimed below at the maniacal mech. Then I shot off another grenade.

You know, it's funny, I'd seen this maneuver done in a movie once. I've also fantasized about doing this maneuver in my wildest nerd dreams. But I got to say that the landing, you know, that thing that happens after you leap from a bullet-ridden twelve story building, was never part of my fantasies.

After that day I knew why. Because when you jump off a twelve-story building, no matter how drenched with bodacity, no matter what you do in the air, there isn't really a way to land that's not riddled with pain and sorrow.

I got to hand it to whoever made the S-16, though. Those things can take a beating.

My dive kept going after I launched my frag and didn't stop until I crashed through the sixth story window of the opposite building across the street, landing hard on my armored stomach and skidding almost twenty feet before stopping when my helmet connected with the leg of a coffee table.

I don't really remember the words I said as I climbed to my hands and knees. Just as well because it was probably something wimpy.

Then my grenade went off. The floor shook beneath me before the entire room collapsed and I fell through a few levels before stopping on what I was guessing was the third or fourth floor of the crumbling building.

Hoping Chloe was well away from the S-20 when it went

boom would have been on my mind just then had not, after I got to my feet again, the building started to teeter.

It's really hard to explain the feeling of being inside a collapsing building, so here's my best analogy: it's like being inside a large wooden box falling into an active volcano and scraping along the walls all the way down.

Got a good mental pic? Good. Now throw me, the hero of this tale, in the same mental pic yelling, sweating, and running in crazy slow-motion toward the nearest window as the pitch of the floor rises more and more until I'm running up an almost vertical surface by the time I break through the icy glass.

I didn't really fly through gracefully so, while you got that mental pic still rolling around in your little noggin, picture me, screaming like a banshee and running on the now almost horizontal brick wall of the building and not quite making it to the bottom when it finally touches down.

Irony wasn't through with me yet, though, and I ended up being right over another window when the building landed and before I knew it, I was back inside the building on a grungy couch looking up at the brick wall.

That fell on top of me.

Ouch.

Ouch more to the situation than the actual feeling because it felt like I was being dog-piled by six year olds more than being buried alive by tons of bricks.

Thank you, S-16, I love you.

Chapter 17

It took Chloe almost five minutes to remove enough rubble for me to poke a hand out and another three to actually pull me out. "Are you injured?" she asked, examining my suit for dents or punctures.

My heart was racing, my mind was buzzing, and my body felt drenched in sweat. But other than that, I could still see and didn't feel like I was about to puke too bad, so I was guessing I wasn't about to die. "I'm good," I told her, climbing to my shaky feet.

Removing my helmet so I could breathe easier, I found a spot in what was left of the apartment and sat down. I ran a metal glove through my soaking hair, spitting out the bile that had started working its way up my throat about halfway between buildings during my leap of faith.

"You okay?" I asked, glancing at her as she removed her helmet, letting her hair, which, might I point out in annoyance, looked extremely dry, shiny, and positively daisy fresh, tumble down as she did so.

"It'll take more than one S-20 piloted by an inexperienced Fascist to kill me," she stated with confidence.

"I would've settled for you at least breaking a sweat," I muttered. "So that means the Fascists control Flagstaff?"

Chloe, who didn't have to sit down to regain her composure like me, took this time to reload her assault rifle. "Not at all. Neither the Bears nor Fascists have control of Flagstaff. Both parties would rather keep it that way since it's occupied by the Reds and is completely neutral in the war."

"And thus can sell the weapons no doubt being created here to both sides," I finished.

Chloe smiled at me as she cocked her rifle. "Just so. Since it would cost more time and men to seize the city for both sides than to just buy what they need, the Reds are left to their own devices."

"Not to mention that a failed attempt for control would most likely result in the Reds joining up with the other side and cutting off trade rights," I said, getting a surprised smile from Chloe.

"That's amazing," was all she said. Her smile was saying the rest.

Now, if I could only keep up the act of being a freakishly knowledgeable philanthropist instead of some geek who had been betrayed by the French one too many times on Medieval II: Total War, then I'd be looking better all the time.

"You're a Red?" I asked, standing and starting to reload my rifle.

"Proudly," Chloe said. "We represent the very heart of Russia with our hard work, engineering, and love for her people."

"Let me guess. The Fascists have the morals and religious ideas, the Bears have the firepower and stubborn streak and you guys fix everything that breaks because the other two sides put too much time into morals and power, right?"

Chloe frowned, rolling her eyes around a little in thought before finally saying, "That's pretty much it."

I nodded knowingly. "Just so you know, I always chose the industrious sides in every online game that came down the pike."

Chloe didn't really know what to say to that as we made our way back to the street where what was left of the S-20 smoldered away in chunks. I asked her what he'd been doing there and why he decided to attack us since we were wearing Fascist armor and all.

That little inquiry induced a ten-minute lecture that brought me up to speed on the difference between actual Fascists, which was what the S-20 had been, and Rogues, which was what the guys who had dropped an EMP grenade into my 2340 welcome packet had been. Also, somewhere in the lecture she told me that we actually needed to get out of our current armor ASAP because no one liked the Rogues due to their knack for ambushing convoys from all sides and preying on the weak. Her final answer about why the S-20 had been there was most likely to buy fuel.

"If you love this junk," Chloe said as we slunk through the streets, waving at my armor. "Then you should get a real rush out of my father's new design christened the Dragunov. They haven't become available for combat as of yet, but when they do they'll cost right at one-hundred-million holos a unit."

"What's a holo?" I asked.

"Eh, the digital equivalent to one ruble."

I was shocked at the price at first until I remembered that ruble was way different from good old U.S. bucks and that one-hundred-million ruble was right around $3,406,251 for us.

And fifteen cents.

"Can your daddy's new Dragunov run as fast as these?" I asked, stepping into yet another alleyway behind Chloe.

"Actually, they have only been clocked at forty miles per hour at top speed."

I nodded, not really sure where her dad had made this crazy breakthrough that I was supposedly going to "get a rush out of" if forty mph was all I could get out of his new design. Then Chloe sealed the deal by smiling at me and saying, "But it can fly over two-hundred."

See? Isn't the future flipping great? I had a feeling that Dr. Atrium Sparks and I were going to get along just fine.

After we had found a suitably abandoned shack, Chloe decided that ditching our suits would be best done now rather than later, stating that we shouldn't push our luck.

After we'd got out of the suits and I had started jumping around like a loser with chattering teeth, Chloe went through the rooms in search of spoils. I was guessing the shack had once been a gas station of sorts then later someone had moved into it in its present mutilated state and had attempted to wall in a few sections for privacy.

"In here," Chloe called to me from one of the makeshift rooms. I waddled in, trying to keep my legs close together like I'd seen some penguins do in documentaries, thinking that this would help with the cold. It didn't.

Being soaked with sweat had been fine in the S-16 but not so much in the bitter freezing elements of Flagstaff. Just how cold was it, anyway?

"It's only ten below," Chloe told me after seeing my march of the penguins dance and somehow reading my mind. "Stop being such a wimp," she said, waving at a trunk she'd found. "Let's see what we can find us to wear."

I was shocked at how fruitful our search had been. Shocked and super grateful to whoever had left the trunk.

Once we'd finished pulling on the clothes we looked like a couple of mercenaries. The thick plain black shirts and pants weren't the snazziest apparel but the heavy dark red overcoats that reached to our knees were pretty much wicked. Thick, too.

Since Chloe hadn't sweated like an Egyptian slave in her suit, she didn't have to take off any soaked clothing like yours truly. I stripped down to my boxers, which were staying no matter how drenched they were, and pulled on the black pants, dropping my beloved Amosu on the floor, never to be picked up again.

Then I noticed Chloe looking at me.

"What?" I asked. "I'm not about to put on some dead dude's undies." Since I seem to lack the general part of the brain that tells the mouth to stop while it's ahead, I finished with, "Just be glad you got to see this much. I once dated a chick for eight months in college who never even saw my feet."

I'm guessing she didn't think I noticed her and, to be honest, I didn't at first. I mean, Jericho Johnson had just taken off his shirt in the presence of a woman. Of course she was staring. And possibly even drooling like a blood-hound. Not sure because I wasn't close enough to tell.

Alright, I'm kidding. I mean, for a guy my age and build, you'd think I'd be a little more cut but, sadly, I'm not. I don't look like someone in the last stage of leukemia, or anything, just not exactly built. I've been told I'm appealing but not exactly hot. Hope that sums up my body to you because that's all I've got.

"You're really tan for a guy who spends most of his time in a basement," Chloe said.

And tan. Did I mention I had a nice tan going on for me?

Alright, I lied, again. What was actually said was, "Wow, but you're pale. Don't you ever leave that basement of yours?"

"Says the milky-white Russian chick that lives on Lost Planet," I shot back, pulling on my shirt.

I didn't notice the patch on the right arm of our new coats until I saw Chloe pull on the red overcoat. "Please tell me there aren't any Nazis left."

Chloe blinked at me for a second before noticing me point to the Swastika on my sleeve. She frowned at hers before saying, "We did have a lot of stuff stolen from one of our museums below. I suppose whoever broke in must have stashed some of it here."

"So," I said, slinging my assault rifle on my back, "We're not going to get lynched for wearing these?"

"Not at all," she said, picking up her rifle. "If anything they'll think we robbed the museum and we'll be arrested."

Try and get a good picture of us, if you can. Chloe looked halfway decent because all she really added to her black jumpsuit and heeled boots was the long, rusty-red Nazi coat. I, on the other hand, looked like a coloring book in the same coat with my black Chuck's still on my feet.

And think what you want but the Nazis had some snappy uniforms. I know it's not cool to say but they really did.

"Why're we sneaking in, anyway?" I asked. "I mean, this is where you live, right? Can't we just walk right up and knock on the door?"

I fell in step behind Chloe as we exited the hovel. "We can't. Verde von Klaus has my father deep below the city so that's where we're going. Giving Klaus the glove would make everything my father has done obsolete."

"But it's to save his life," I stated. "Not to point out the elephant in the room, but I thought that we were going to hand it over anyway. Regardless of what your old man thought."

Chloe didn't answer for a long time as we made our way through the abandoned streets. The snow had picked up since we left the hovel, and I noticed the white flakes looked nice adorning the back of Chloe's head, her jet black hair swaying back and forth while she walked.

"I've thought about it," she said finally, making me have to remember what we'd even been talking about to start with. Oh yeah, handing the glove over.

"And you've decided against it?" I asked, glancing at the dead gauntlet I was wearing on my right hand.

"Yes," was all she said.

We walked in more silence for a while before I asked, "Won't Klaus be a little agitated if he finds out you're double-crossing him?"

"Yes."

"Like, kill us kind of agitated?"

"Yes."

More silence as we trudged the white streets.

Oh, well. I suppose that if I did get killed by some crazy, rich, Russian guy then I could go out of this life knowing that I died while trying to help a wicked hot girl save her father's life.

Yeah. Forget that crap. I wanted to live.

I was about to let Chloe know that maybe I could just go back to the hovel and wait it out with my gun when she said, "You don't have to come, Jericho. There really isn't a need for both of us to die if it comes to that."

She had a point. No need for two people to die if one would be just as...

Wait.

If I quit now, I'd look like more of a wimp than I would have if it had been my idea. But now it would just seem like Chloe was like, I don't know, letting me out of my end of the deal.

I'm so glad that Chloe wasn't able to hear all those

thoughts I just told you about because they only lasted in reality around ten seconds, just enough time for me to say, "Whatever, woman. You know you'd be lost without me."

And that was that.

Any thoughts you may have had about my throwing in the towel can be trashed, whoever-you-are, because Jericho Johnson was going to see this possibly horrible train wreck through to the end.

Chapter 18

We hadn't walked five more minutes when we reached the entrance to what Chloe called the bunker, letting me know that we were about to enter a labyrinth of shadowed halls and creepiness but not to worry because she had been this way before.

When she was eight.

And with her dad.

After receiving this little tidbit, I said, "Sure thing, Chloe. Why would I worry about getting lost in a labyrinth of shadowy halls in Russian-occupied America wearing Nazi memorabilia?"

Whether Chloe didn't hear me or just decided to ignore my wit, I wasn't sure. Either way she didn't answer. She squatted down in front of me and started fanning her gloved hands around on the concrete of the alley, brushing away the snow to reveal a manhole.

Together, only after I'd let her try herself for almost a whole minute, we pried the lid up. I was expecting the smell of a sewer but instead received a full blast in the face that smelled like Lysol and lots of the stuff.

"You never said anything about breaking into a Dollar General," I said, covering my nose. "Seriously, I think my nose hairs just burnt off."

"Stop being a baby, Jericho. It's just sterilization," she told me before dropping into the blackness.

"I actually plan on having kids one day, Chloe," I called down into the dark.

"Not that kind of sterilization, idiot," I heard her say, her voice echoing.

Hoping she was right, I dropped in behind her. Upon landing, Chloe then told me that the manhole had to be closed. I peered up at the opening almost eight feet above us and said,

"Sure thing. I'll get on your shoulders."

I was joking, of course, and Chloe realized this, stating that if I couldn't hold her she'd understand. "Shut up," I said, lacing my fingers for a handhold, to which Chloe accepted, and in a few seconds she was sitting on my shoulders.

"Don't bother hurrying, dear," I grunted. "You're light as a feather."

Once the manhole was back in place it was dark. Like, severely dark. Like, darker than black type dark.

"So," I said casually, "this seems like a bad idea."

Chloe laughed at that, climbing down from my shoulders. "Just be glad it's summer or else we'd have to worry about ice spiders."

"How cold is the wintertime?" I asked, a little shocked that ten below was deemed summertime.

"Almost negative eighty most of the time. Access to the surface is only done with mechs, and even then only for short periods at a time because they will freeze up." I heard her rummaging around in the darkness before hearing a slight crack and seeing that Chloe had produced an almost foot-long glow stick.

I fell in step behind Chloe as she started making her way down the damp underground tunnel. "And what're ice spiders?"

I saw her silhouette shrug. "Just big spiders that normally live above until it gets too cold. Then they move down here for the winter."

I was surprised, shocked, astounded, and frankly, a little scared. I mean, I'd killed as many ice spiders as anyone else who has played any standard role-playing game, but I always hoped that if any fantasy creatures were ever real, giant man-eating spiders wouldn't be one of them.

"How, uh, big are we talking, here?" I asked as nonchalantly as possible.

"Depends," she said. "Up top they can range from four feet across, which is an infant and not at all a danger, to the big ones which can get up to ten feet across."

I made a sort of fluttery whining sound that was completely involuntary. I mean, call me crazy, but four feet wide spiders sounded pretty darn big to me.

"Whatever," I said, coughing like I needed to clear my throat and stepping around a puddle. "I'm just glad we won't be running into any. Just so you know, spiders we in 2012 classify as big are, like, ten inches across. And those are the monster ones."

Chloe just nodded, and I was glad she didn't decide to tell me that there were also killer snakes bigger than redwood trees or cockroaches the size of German shepherds lurking around here in the dark.

I don't remember how long we walked then, with Chloe making the occasional right or left turn and me close behind just in case she was wrong about the great ice spider migration. After what seemed an eternity, with my mind playing tricks on me with shadows and my mind also showing me vivid pictures of having the flesh torn from my face by savage spiders, I opened my mouth to ask Chloe if, by any crazy chance, summer was almost over and if winter was coming then—

Then I ran into her because she had stopped walking.

I thought she'd stopped because Shelob herself was blocking our path, so I silently peered around Chloe, and then sighed with relief when I saw that it wasn't Shelob but only a dead end.

"Wrong turn?" I asked.

Chloe dropped to her knees and began brushing away at the floor like she'd done in the alley and within seconds had found yet another trapdoor.

The two of us went to work to get it open and did, but with a lot more effort than the time before. Once we were done we both ended up sitting back and panting a little.

"Geez, this hatch has been shut a while," I said, trying to catch my breath.

Chloe nodded and got to her knees. "Since I was eight," she confirmed, looking down the hole. "This one has lights so we won't need this," she said, tossing the glow stick aside. "We're almost where they're keeping my father. He's only guarded by two guards, which change every twelve hours."

"So we just walk in and bump the guys on the head?" I asked, hoping that wasn't the plan.

"More or less. We need to get in their armor. The problem is the surveillance cameras. Three, actually."

I peered at Chloe in the dim light. I could tell she hadn't thought this part of the plan through. Or, if she did, she hadn't thought about it too hard. "We can't cut power to the cameras?"

"Won't work," Chloe said, shaking her head. "The guards will be able to see us in the dark with their helmets."

I stood and offered a hand to her. "Well, I'm all out of ideas."

Chloe accepted my hand, getting to her feet. "We'll try to draw the guards into a dead zone and subdue them. It's possible, just more dangerous."

I held up my hands. "After the mammoth mech in the streets, I'm ready for some normal dudes. Mitch taught me some stuff, so I know tai-jutsu, nin-jutsu, and jiujutsu."

"As do I," Chloe said. "Haven't used them much, but I had the skills implanted just in case. I prefer to shoot people."

"Too bad the gloves are out of commission," I said, glancing at my dead glove that I was wearing. "I bet we could've shocked the crap out of those guys."

Chloe started explaining to me about the closest dead zone that didn't have any cameras which was close enough to the guards to get their attention and draw them away. One would probably stay behind, but after we knocked out his pal we hoped he'd run to his rescue.

Chloe's final hope was that whoever was watching the screen the camera was feeding to would see two guards leave and two return. Easy.

We dropped into the opening and landed quietly on the marble floor. Yeah, you heard right. Marble floor. It looked like we'd just dropped into a fancy hospital with the same sterile smell in the air. It took a while for our eyes to adjust to the brightness before Chloe gave me the sign for silence and we began creeping down the brightly lit hallway.

It felt kind of stupid to be sneaking down a bright hallway, actually, but I wasn't about to question Chloe's motives. She had been here before, after all, whereas I was just the handsome tag-a-long. Before long the hallway made a sudden right and Chloe squatted down and motioned me down beside her. With our backs to the wall a few inches away from the edge, Chloe produced a pocket mirror and checked around the corner.

After she'd finished her cliché reconnaissance she glanced at me, grabbed my head softly, and pulled my ear against her lips. "They are both there," she whispered, her words vibrating on my right lobe and her breath feeling warm against my cold ear.

Since she wasn't exactly worrying her pretty little head about the closeness, I leaned in and pressed my lips to her ear. "Then go ahead, girl scout," I whispered. "I'm right behind you," then, because I really wasn't caring about blowing my cover at that point, I said, "You smell really good, by the way."

Chloe pulled away, checked her mirror one last time, glanced at me then pulled my ear to her lips again. "Thanks," she said and I could feel the smile on her lips. "You don't smell so bad yourself."

Then, before I could tell her thank you, she stood suddenly, pulling me up with her. Taking a few steps back, Chloe then proceeded to stomp really hard, the noise echoing down the hallway like a gunshot.

It took a few fractured seconds for me to realize that she had just alerted the guards to our presence and that we should probably run. Darting back the way we'd came, our footsteps rang out almost as loud as Chloe's little heel stomp, so if there were any question the guards might have had about intruders, they were now confirmed.

We heard them discuss something for a second before hearing two sets of footsteps coming our way.

Chloe flipped off a light switch when we ran into the last

stretch of hallway that led to our ceiling entrance. The rest of this little scene didn't take too long and, honestly, not to sound like the snail that was mugged by the turtle, but it all happened so fast.

The future was a dangerous place. Of course, now that I look back on it, I suppose you could argue that breaking into any maximum security facility could get you shot no matter what year it was. This place wasn't exactly Langley or anything, but I was thinking these guys weren't playing around.

And neither was Chloe.

The first guard to round the corner received what I could only discern as a perfect ten hurricane kick to the side of his helmet, causing him to stagger and crash into the opposite wall. I was so mesmerized by Chuck Norris's daughter that I forgot about the other guard, who hadn't forgotten about me and grabbed me up in a painful bear hug and started squeezing the life out of me before I knew what was happening.

Normally, grabbing someone and squeezing them really hard wasn't exactly one of the best moves a guy could try. I mean, he could get his eyes gouged out, his ears bitten off— you know, rough stuff. Unless, of course, the hugger happens to be wearing a super advanced battle suit, then the hug is pretty much lethal and his head is protected by a helmet.

I was glad I couldn't breathe or else I would've screamed like a little girl for madam ninja to save me. Not that it would've made much difference considering I saw that Chloe had somehow gotten the other guard's helmet off and was pounding his face with it.

I struggled against the strong arms clamped around me and kicked my feet around like crazy. I managed to somehow swivel a little, just enough to plant both my boots against the wall and push off as hard as I could, tripping my attacker and landing on top of him as we both fell to the hard marble floor.

Feeling air rush into my lungs when he lost his grip on me, I rolled off of him quickly and mounted his chest, grabbing at his mask in a desperate attempt to remove it so I could bludgeon his fat head like Chloe had done.

I was guessing the guard wasn't exactly digging the idea of my bludgeoning him with his own helmet because all it took to remove me from his chest was for him to grab my coat collar and throw me into the air.

Okay, I know you guys out there are probably realists. I mean, I know you probably want to hear this action-packed story about my heroic feats and stuff. But, I also know that you guys aren't going to take a lot of what I say to heart. Mainly about all the wild, crazy, gravity defying things that have happened already and are going to happen later.

But let me go ahead and tell you that everything is completely true.

Alright, moving on. Just figured you needed to know that before I tell this next part.

The guard sent me flying into the air like a badminton birdie and crashing through the thin ceiling. Pain shot through my left leg as the thin aluminum panels that made up the ceiling bit through my pants and into skin. My ride wasn't finished as I cart wheeled three times in the open attic space, yelling like an idiot, before crashing through the ceiling again almost ten feet away from where I'd ripped through.

I landed on all fours, which resulted in my face planting the marble floor from the force. I lay there for a few seconds, with my cheek against the cold floor and noticed that it was quiet. Groaning, I rolled over to check on who was winning.

The guard that'd just thrown me like a ragdoll was lying lifeless on the floor, his helmet removed and a pool of blood seeping out from under his head. Chloe was standing between the two downed guards with a helmet in each hand. "You alright?" she asked.

"Never better," I gasped out. "But I think I may have just crapped my pants."

Chloe crossed over to me. "These suits are pretty tough. I guess maybe I was expecting less action, though."

"Sorry to be the burden of high-flying action," I muttered,

extending a hand. Once I was pulled up my head started spinning. I told you that I cart wheeled three times because that seemed more logical, but to be honest, I'm not sure how many times I really spun in the air before my landing.

Three. Yeah, we'll say three.

Chapter 19

"Try not to act like a child when we get back in range of the cameras," Chloe's voice buzzed in my helmet. "And don't make any sudden movements, either. Soldiers actually train for a whole year before wearing a Raptor-6."

I nodded, smiling like a maniac, glad that she couldn't see my face. These suits made the previous suits we'd worn look like complete junk. The HUD, or heads up display for the people not familiar with gaming phraseology, had almost 180 degree vision. A small diagram was floating to the bottom right of my sight, indicating the condition of the suit. We didn't have to take our coats off before donning the suits, but we had to lose our gauntlets of time, stashing them in a small compartment on the right side of the suit's chest piece.

I was almost a foot taller in the Raptor-6, making me feel like I was walking on stilts, but I wasn't really caring as I strutted around in the dark red steel suit.

"Where're the weapons on these things?" I asked, just noticing that the guards hadn't actually been toting any guns when we attacked them.

"These haven't been outfitted yet," Chloe said. "Normally there are two shoulder Gatlings, unless you wanted to put your grenade launcher on one shoulder, which is really more of an infantry thing. Most soldiers prefer to have the launcher in the right knee, which works like a mortar when kneeling," holding up her left arm, she said, "Sub-machine guns are generally installed in the forearms and work with the suits auto-lock capability, which will make your arms move for you. Not a good feeling at first but people learn to deal with it."

We turned the corner, now in sight of the cameras. "Did they just not figure on needing weapons down here?" I asked.

"Yes. My father abhors guns."

We reached the metal door and Chloe instantly started punching in numbers on the keypad. "If anything out of the ordinary happens, the guards check on my father," she said as the door slid open. I'm guessing she said that little tidbit to set my mind at ease, but I could so tell she was really trying to set her own mind at ease.

The room was enormous. For a laboratory, I mean. And the silence was pretty noticeable, too. Amongst all the tables that littered the room overflowing with all kinds of science stuff that I didn't recognize, and that's coming from a guy who basically lives in his lab in his basement, I got my first look at Chloe's dad.

I don't really know what I had been expecting about Dr. Atrium Sparks. Maybe a little like a mad scientist but nothing too much more than that. All I know is that Dr. Atrium Sparks didn't fit my previous conceptions at all.

First off, his hair wasn't white or even graying but instead jet black. Secondly, he was a flipping beast. He looked like a body-builder with glasses and a lab coat. Chloe had removed her helmet by then and her dad saw her, and in a split seconds they were in each other's arms.

"Clover, I'm so glad you're safe," he told her, looking the same size as the suit she was wearing, which was ridiculous. "I was beginning to think you were dead."

Since I hadn't exactly been invited to the tearful reunion, I decided I'd check out the lab while they were having a good cry. That is, until I actually took a step and Dr. Sparks noticed me and produced a handgun.

"Who are you?" he growled, his deep lovable father voice gone.

Sadly, this wasn't the first time I'd met a girl's father only to have him threaten me with a gun. Her name had been Raven Collins and her daddy was an ex-marine with a severe love for his daughter and firearms.

I was fifteen at the time. Remember how I said I hated that number?

"He's with me, father," Chloe decided to say, only after her old man had already made me feel about as unwelcome as he could. "He's also the finder of the glove."

Upon hearing his daughter's words, Dr. Sparks gasped, dropping his gun like it had burned him. Removing my helmet, I crossed over to him and held out an armored hand. "Pleased to make your acquaintance, Doctor. I'm—"

"Jericho Johnson," he said suddenly, "from 2012." He was still holding his hand like it was burned and his brows had furrowed in deep thought. He was also staring at me in disbelief.

"Your butler's name is Evonne, your maid's name is Louise, you're a history professor, celebrity, and billionaire who met my daughter the first time in Rome in A.D. 98 on a Thursday."

Now it was my turn for disbelief. "How do you know any of that? Have we met?"

"Only once," he said, taking a step toward me. "When I'd first finished the glove, I tried jumping forward a few years as a test. You were here in Flagstaff during a revolt." His eyes were glassy in an almost drunk like way, and I saw him swallow as a bead of sweat rolled down his cheek.

Something was up. Either this dude wasn't right upstairs, had a weak heart, or wasn't telling me everything. I was thinking the latter.

"What happened?" I asked.

"We met topside," he said, each word seeming like a struggle. "I had only known you for a few minutes maybe, when..."

"When what?" I asked, my voice rising in panic.

"There was an explosion in the southern precinct," Dr. Sparks said. "You died there, Jericho."

I didn't say anything, choosing instead to keep looking at him hard.

"I saw what was left of your body," he said, staring intently at me. "You were dead, son."

"Why was I there? Who was with me?" I said, my voice

sounding loud in my own ears.

"You said you didn't have time to explain. The things I told you about yourself were the only things you told me then to prove that you were from the past. My only assumption was you told me that just for this meeting right now."

I'm going to pause this tale a minute to explain a plan I had made on one of my first voyages. The plan, as elaborate as I'd like to say it was, was merely just a line or phrase that I used almost everywhere for instances just like this when verifying my credibility was a life or death situation.

Of course, you know, I never, like, thought about the whole life or death thing too literally.

For those of you who have been listening intently like I hope you have, you might actually remember the plan when you hear it. Maybe.

"Did I say something to you or ask you something that sounded a little crazy?" I asked the doctor.

"What? No, I don't think—ah!" he said, snapping his fingers. "Yes, you did, as a matter of fact," he pursed his lips in thought and screwed one eye closed as he pondered, causing me to wonder if this guy really was one of the great minds of his age like everyone thought. "I believe you asked what my thoughts were on global warming and some sort of epidemic, or something."

"The mad cow disease," I said, my shoulders sagging.

"Yes, that's it," Dr. Sparks said, smiling because I'm guessing he had been trying to remember it for a while. Then he noticed my face and also the gravity of what he'd just told me.

"Yeah," I said, nodding once and pointing. "I'm going to go clear my head on the other side of this rather depressing lab. It was a blast meeting you, doc," I started towards the opposite side of the lab, which, might I point out, turned out to be rocking an equal dose of depression. "Let's do this again sometime."

Chapter 20

While I was wallowing in self-pity, Chloe told her father about the glove situation. "Where is the original?" he asked her. Sighing, because clearly they couldn't last two minutes without me, I opened up my chest piece.

"Here," I said, holding out the glove, which, unless the good doctor was wrong, was going to be the harbinger of my inevitable and extremely untimely demise.

Dr. Sparks took the glove and turned it over in his hands. "When did you notice it wasn't working?"

I was about to delve into seemingly the most sarcastic uncalled for response I've ever tried but Chloe, who knew me well enough to know that I wasn't in the best of moods, cut me off. "Almost ten or fifteen minutes after the EMP grenade."

Dr. Sparks sat at his desk and in seconds had opened the glove. All thoughts of my death and being ticked about it vanished when I saw him crack open the glove. "How'd you do that?" I asked. "I've been trying to open that thing for months."

"I designed it to only open for me," he said, pointing to a spot on the glove casing that looked basically like the rest of the glove. "It recognizes my impression here, thus allowing me, and only me, access. Were the gauntlet able to be opened by just anyone we would have a few more problems than we already do."

"You mean like dying? Because that sounds like a big one," then I looked at him. "Did you just call it a gauntlet?"

Nodding, Dr. Sparks looked thoughtfully at his life's work in his hands, "Yes. I've always thought it resembled a gauntlet more than a glove."

"Yeah, me too," I said, excited that I wasn't the only loser left on the planet. "Why'd you give it sharp fingers, anyway?"

Opening the gauntlet more to expose the innards, he said, "The design to fit the required components left it with only one dangerously sharp finger, so I decided to make the others match. Tell me, did they ever come in handy?"

Shrugging, I said, "At times. Killed a man in the second crusade with them once."

Dr. Sparks was livid. "Y-you killed someone with them?"

"How was I supposed to know they were just for looks?" I shot at him. "They're flipping sharp, man."

I leaned over his shoulder to get a better look at gauntlet guts. "Where's all the, uh, you know," I started, frowning in confusion as my voice trailed off.

"The actual science stuff?" Dr. Sparks asked.

He was right. I had been expecting wires, smallish motherboard looking things, and, well, more wires. What I saw instead was a little odd. The only wiring and hardware located inside had to do with the touch-screen and that was it, really, except for one lone red wire that went from the touch-screen to something that resembled a palm-sized garnet that was glowing bright blue and looking expensive.

Dr. Sparks lifted the glowing garnet out of the case it was snuggly residing in and detached the wire, which was inserted into what I was guessing was a bored hole in the garnet

Holding it up for us to see, except he was looking at it in wonder like he'd never lain eyes on the thing before, he said, "It's all about this, you know. This is what has made our conversation today possible, Jericho Johnson."

"And my untimely death, don't forget," I muttered but my sarcasm wasn't heard by the man who was staring wonderingly at the garnet. "So what is it, exactly?"

"I call it element Z-90, but who knows what it really is," he said.

"Well, since you've developed a way to travel through time with it, I was kind of thinking that you did."

"Oh, not in the least," Dr. Sparks told me quickly. "One of the reasons is that what you see here, with the exception of two slivers removed to power the other gauntlets, is the only element zero on the planet to date."

"I'm guessing since it's still glowing, it's not broken or anything?" I asked, peering at it. "Because, you know, I was kind of thinking about some sushi tacos."

Shaking his head, Dr. Sparks said, "No, it's not damaged. We've discerned through some of the first trial testing with Z-90 that shattering a diamond would be easier than cracking it. The screens are the only things that need to be fixed. I wanted to originally design them to work with a holotab but needed more of a remote access," then, cocking his head to the side, he asked, "Sushi tacos?"

Since I didn't feel like explaining my vices to him, I cut to the chase by turning to Chloe and saying, "Alright, Chloe, here's your daddy, safe and sound. Now can I please go home?"

Call it what you will, but I'd had enough of the future to last me the rest of my life. See why I always preferred the past over the unknown?

Chloe then proceeded to explain the whole tale to her father, from my offering to help her save him, to the EMP grenade incident, sparing no detail save some of the awkward moments I know she had when faced with my hotness. Anyway, after story time, which lasted almost five minutes, Dr. Sparks told us a tale of his own. One that included, but was not limited to, murder, espionage, the end of the world and, let's not forget, my death.

And time-travel, too. Yeah, that was mentioned more than once.

"Verde von Klaus is planning something," he started. "I knew from the beginning not to get involved with him but the finances that my research required, a severely vast sum that he was willing to provide…" his voice trailed off.

"Surely there's more to this Klaus guy besides money," I said, leaning against a table and folding my arms.

"He never explained his reasons for wanting to fund my work, though he implied that he had a passion for knowledge in any field," Dr. Sparks said, and he looked like he was going to be sick.

"After the construction of the first gauntlet and successful jump, I went to Klaus to tell him, but I stopped at his office door long enough to overhear a delicate conversation he was having with a colleague."

Chloe was on the edge of her seat, which confused me until I remembered her telling me she didn't know the full extent of Klaus's plan.

"Please understand, Jericho, that the world you knew before is gone. Russia used to have morals once long ago and you may have seen some of them. But when worlds change, so do the occupants. Russia now controls over half the planet and Klaus is at the helm."

"Whoa, back up," I said, holding up my hands. "So he's like a, what, president? King? Dictator for life? I thought he was just some rich guy."

"I'm sure by now you know of the current war between the Fascists and Bears?" he asked.

I nodded.

"Klaus hasn't thrown his lot in with either party so far, not even the Reds," Dr. Sparks said, and he seemed like the thought troubled him. "The conversation I overheard cleared it all up."

He sighed, and Chloe and I watched him. We were probably both thinking, "What the heck, man? Hurry up with the juiciness, already." I know that's what I was thinking right about then.

"To make a long story short, Klaus is planning on sending millions of troops back to 1900."

Chloe frowned, not sure why this was a horrible plot of death and destruction.

But guess what the guy who had a master's degree in history had to say to that?

"It's for 1907," I said plainly, causing Chloe to turn her confused frown on me.

"That's seven years later," she said. "Why not just send them to 1907?"

My eyes never left Dr. Sparks as Klaus's plan, which only

took the few words from Chloe's father to spark, unrolled in my mind. "Because 1900 has plenty of warm bodies, and I'll bet he's not sending thousands of troops. He's sending thousands of these bad boys," I said, tapping the suit I was wearing. "He wants the past soldiers to be fully ready, thus the seven-year gap."

"Ready for what?" Chloe asked in an exasperated tone.

I'm a bit of a freak when it comes to history. Words can't explain how much I adore it. Those reasons, among a few others, are mainly why I'm kind of a walking history book. So, without rushing too much, I spilled the Russian beans to Chloe.

"In 1879 Germany formed a Dual Alliance with Austria-Hungary which later, in 1882, expanded to a Triple Alliance to include Italy with the understanding to support each other if either countries were attacked by France or Russia. Since the French don't like things they don't understand, they felt threatened by this, and with the growth of the German Navy in 1904, so did England. The two countries made an Entente Cordiale, which means friendly understanding. Three years later, with fear of the rising numbers in the German ranks, Russia got in on the no-Germans-allowed club and the Triple Entente was established," the words poured out of me like water.

"What difference does it make?"

"Geez, would someone get this girl a flipping map?" I said, getting too caught up in my rant. "Germany, Austria-Hungary, and Italy are all connected and separate Russia from Britain and France. This alliance was the best thing that ever happened to Russia, who, might I add, also added Serbia to the alliance so Austria-Hungary wouldn't expand their borders."

I had long since started pacing, which was something I tended to do when explaining, well, anything. Blame it on being a college professor. "Industrial unrest in Russia started in 1907 and, as you might know, was Russia's honey-hole, so to speak. The Lena goldfield massacre of 1912, which involved hundreds of uprising striking miners, was Russia's last attempt at stability, and in the first half of 1914, almost half of the industrial workforce was on strike. But at the dawn of the First World War,

Russia started doing what Russia did best."

I stopped long enough to look at my very Russian audience and said, "No offense."

They both shrugged and I kept going.

"Russia was, without a doubt, the largest military powerhouse at the time. We're talking almost six and a half million troops. The problem occurred because they spent so much time building an incredibly large army, and since half the workers were on strike, they didn't have the proper roads or railways for adequate transportation. General Alexander Samsonov, leader of the Russian Second Army, squared off against Germany's General Paul von Hindenburg and General Erich Ludendorff on August 22nd and after six days of slaughter, even with their vast numbers, Russia was surrounded. Samsonov tried to escape, losing most of his men in the process. In the end, only ten thousand of the one-hundred and fifty-thousand Russians escaped, and the Germans, who had lost twenty-thousand men, marched over ninety-two-thousand Russian prisoners off the field. General Samsonov committed suicide afterward."

After spilling all this, I finally got to my point.

"In less than a year after that battle, Russia lost over two-million soldiers and several cities to the German invasion. Not to mention the agricultural bust Russia suffered, which delved what was left of the remaining populace into vast food shortages. Bottom line is, if Samsonov would've won the Battle of Tannenberg, Russia would've most likely won the war. Crushing Germany would've been nothing considering how large the armies were. Once Germany was taken, Austria-Hungary and Italy would've fallen right in line to the new rulers. There really wouldn't have been a limit to the things Russia could've accomplished had Samsonov won."

Silence followed. Chloe seemed to be staring at the floor really hard while her dad did something similar to the opposite wall.

"That's got to be the only logical thing Klaus would be doing," I said. "There could be a slight chance that he just wants to get a mail-order bride, but I wouldn't bet on it."

This was meant as a light attempt at humor to, you know, lighten the mood.

It didn't work.

"So let's recap, shall we?" I started, tapping my suit of armor. "How many of these can you produce in a day?"

"Two-thousand is our daily limit if pushed," Dr. Sparks said. "Although we haven't actually made any in almost two years because we massed produced them and stored almost four million below—" He stopped talking. I'm guessing the real gravity of Klaus's plot just hit him in the face with a glass of ice water.

"No kidding. Four-million?" I echoed, nodding at him. "So he grabs an ungodly amount of firepower, heads back in time to drop it off, and gives them over a decade to train. Any chances of him bringing something back to make railroads and highways?"

Dr. Sparks looked at me. "I suppose he could."

"That's what I would do."

"If he takes the Dragonovs, he won't need any roads," Dr. Sparks said, standing to his feet. "This is why the gauntlet had to be hidden, Jericho. I wasn't able to tell Chloe any of this after Klaus's men took me into custody and she was sent to retrieve it. Had she known, it would not be here now."

"Look, doc," I said. "I feel like the butterfly effect is a bogus theory, but I have to tell you, I haven't really done anything too drastic."

"Such as?" he asked, clearly worried.

"Oh, you know, not too much."

"He punched Leonardo da Vinci in the face," Chloe said, crossing her arms. "And stole a certain Roman emperor's fiddle."

"Yeah, like I said, not much. But changing the course of history this drastic doesn't sound good, if I may say so. No offense, but we beat the Germans. Twice. I don't know what we would've done about you guys."

Dr. Sparks turned to his desk. "Neither do I," was all he said. "I'll fix the gloves, then Chloe will take you home. You've done all you can."

"Just like that?" I asked. "I mean, tell me about impending doom and then send me home?"

"It's not your problem, Jericho," Chloe said.

"Forgive me if I'm incorrect, Chloe, but I believe I'm over three-hundred years older than you. If this thing goes south my world is going down first. You think I'm going to go back to my sushi tacos and Xbox and just wait for Mother Russia to appear on my doorstep in unstoppable battle-armor? Not likely. Regardless of what you people might believe, this affects all of us. I'm in it now and I'm not going home."

Chapter 21

How're you hanging with the story so far, whoever-you-are? Is it the good, gripping action tale that you were hoping for? I sure hope so. It'd be a real bummer to find out I went to all this trouble of recording this thing and you weren't having a great time out there.

Anyway, back to it, then.

Chloe was silently pacing on the other side of the room after my rant about helping them save the world, and her father was tinkering with the gloves. Dr. Sparks had started working on mine first, which was fine by me because apparently that was the only one that mattered anyway, it seemed.

I decided that Chloe needed a little cheering up. Sure, she was a big girl strutting around in a suit of super-armor, but everyone needs a hug every now and then.

"So what's the plan, exactly?" I asked her. I know, right? Not exactly the best way to take a girl's mind off of death and destruction. I thought this after I'd already spoken so I tried to avert the question I'd just thrown out by adding, "Because I was kind of thinking that you and I needed to go out sometime and the end of the world would put a big damper on my sweeping you off your feet."

The last two days that I had just spent with Chloe was actually the most time I'd ever spent with one girl, almost. Not saying I was this womanizing player or anything, just stating the facts. Most of the girls I sent packing weren't mean or psychopaths. I just didn't really care to be around them anymore.

The only other girl I'd spent an enormous length of time with was Piper from my trip to the Vikings.

Chloe, on the other hand, was someone who I was thoroughly enjoying being around. Maybe because I can literally count on one hand the small amount of women that I don't mind being around, or that all the other girls thought I was some dude who could tell the future that made them unappealing. I'm not really sure. All I know is that Chloe Sparks knew the real me, with all my flaws, yes, I admit I have a few, and she still hadn't given me the boot, so I'm guessing that she was starting to enjoy my company, too, maybe.

And I don't have that many flaws. Maybe, like, two or three, max.

And I suppose my helping save her daddy was one of the reasons she didn't give me the boot.

Then I was thrown from my thoughts by Chloe saying, "I'm really glad you came, by the way. You didn't have to help me."

I have this weird habit of not being able to hold eye-contact with people who are talking directly to me. It's not that I'm embarrassed, shy or anything. I just can't for some reason. But I'm smart enough to know when eye-contact shouldn't be wavered because of the importance of what whoever is speaking to me is saying.

I turned my head to look at her and, sure enough, she was looking at me. What was I supposed to say? I mean, I wanted to say a lot of stuff but only, like, two of them had anything to do with what she was saying. I was so glad none of my inner-turmoil showed on my face, and I really looked like I was content just staring into her face.

Reaching over, she touched my armored hand with hers. "Thank you," was all she said. Then she was gone, walking to the other side of the room where her father was working on the gauntlets.

And that was pretty much it. I mean, really, Jericho? You couldn't have said, oh, I don't know, anything?

Since I had apparently made her feel better somehow or another, I waited a few minutes, mainly because I didn't want her to think I was following her like a terrier, before crossing the room. "So," I said, "how're the gloves going?"

"The original is finished," Dr. Sparks said, holding up

mine.

I took it from him and turned it over in my hands. "Chloe said there wasn't a plan. So, how would a guy go about making one? Because I'm not digging this whole end-of-the-world thing."

Dr. Sparks stood, "I'm afraid the second glove is useless at least for time-travel. The Z-90 shard was somehow de-energized from the grenade, I'm afraid. Removing a replacement would take days whereas we have an hour, at best."

I frowned. "Hour to do what?"

Then, and I mean, like, right *then* and most certainly not a whole hour away, an alarm went off. Dr. Sparks, who, to me, should have been running around like a madman, simply sighed and said, "Did I say the hour was wishful thinking?"

"Yeah, try like two minutes," I shot at him. "I still don't know what we're supposed to do. I mean, not to sound ungrateful, but you've been a tad vague, doc."

Dr. Sparks walked to the entrance and tapped away at the keypad, closing what looked like a blast shield on the lab side of the door. "This should buy us about ten minutes," he said before smashing the keypad with a hard punch. "Get out of those suits."

Without questioning him, Chloe and I proceeded to remove the armor. They were actually easy to get on and off, which was surprising considering how snug you felt strutting around in them. Dr. Sparks
eyed our Nazi coats for a second before nodding, "I'd heard a museum had been robbed. I suppose they'll be warm if you need them for your jump."

"Jump to where?" I asked, adjusting my long coat.

"We only have minutes, so I need both of you to listen carefully," he said quickly. "Klaus is not without friends. The only chance we have to stop him is two years into the future during a revolt in the middle of the city."

I frowned. This sounded familiar. I raised my hand.

"Question."

"Yes?"

"Would this happen to be the same revolt that I die in?"

Dr. Sparks shrugged apologetically then nodded. "The same."

"So what, I just, uh, avoid anything that blows up? Is that your plan?"

"I was going to say not enter the city, but yes, avoiding exploding objects wouldn't hurt, I'd think," he said. Holding out his hand, he said, "Let me have the gauntlet one last time."

I handed him the glove and looked at Chloe.

"Chloe?"

"Yes?"

"I don't want to die."

Since I said this in a sing-song voice she smiled at me. "Who knows, maybe you'll die before that so you won't have to worry about it."

Since that wasn't what I wanted to hear, I turned back to her father. "Why can't we just kill Klaus before that?"

"Not possible. He's on constant lockdown due to his numerous enemies in high places," Dr. Sparks said, punching away at the gauntlet screen. "But, as luck would have it, Klaus is about to follow the two of you after your jump."

"And this is a good thing how?"

"I've just programmed your glove to use some of your latest jumps as means to lose them. Since I don't know where you have been they can't get anything out of me," he handed me back the gauntlet. "You kill Klaus in the revolt, Jericho, so him going after the two of you will put him right where we need him."

This was going way too fast.

"Slow down a sec," I said. "Let me see if I can try and zero in on your logic. You want me and your daughter to get swept around random places in time so that Klaus will follow us, and I can kill him two years from now?"

It sounded crazy. Like, really crazy. But Dr. Sparks nodded and since I didn't see any other plan in sight, and also since I'd already manned up again to save the world, I just said, "Okay.

Just making sure we were on the same page."

"We won't have any weapons except the gloves," Chloe pointed out.

"Don't worry," I told her. "I know a guy."

Someone pounded hard against the door to the lab and shouted something unintelligible. "That'll be Klaus's men," Dr. Sparks said, seeming almost cavalier about the whole thing. "Clover, could you give me and Jericho a second?"

Chloe was probably more than a little curious as to why her father wanted to have a talk with the guy she'd brought home and so was the guy, actually.

"I know you feel like you don't know what's exactly happening or how to act," he started, looking at me intently. "All I know is, when I met you two years from now, you knew what you had to do. I don't know what happens along the way, but in the end, you hate Klaus more than anything."

I let that sink in for a second, not really liking the sound of it.

"Don't let my daughter out of your sight."

I was about to ask him why when the pounding stopped and the grinding started on the door. Dr. Sparks pulled us into the center of the room and had to shout over the noise from the guards trying to gain entrance. "These jumps are each timed differently," he told us. "When it's time to go you'll have to be together or one of you will get left behind," then, he touched Chloe's arm one last time before rushing to the door to, I don't know, see if he could keep the bad guys out longer, I guess.

Wow. This plan just got more and more half-cocked by the second. We just stood there, not really sure what we were supposed to be doing until I looked at the screen on my glove.

There was a timer on the bottom right hand corner of the screen that was counting down.

It had seven seconds left. Panicking, I grabbed Chloe around the waist with my left arm, pulling her to me as I checked what our destination was.

794 A.D.

"Hope you like Icelandic cod," I told her.

The last thing Chloe said before her face melted away with mine into the fabrics of time and space was, "What's cod?"

Oh, yeah. This was going to be a blast.

That was sarcasm if you didn't catch it the first time.

Chapter 22

Svalbard, January 17, 794 A.D.

For those of you out there who have actually been listening intently, you might recall that my first expedition to the Vikings was in 793 A.D. and not, in fact, 794 A.D.

I guess this is the best time to tell you that I stayed with my brethren of the north almost three months and carried over into the next year.

Also, since we didn't go back to the first time I was in Svalbard, I was thinking that all the jumps would land me back to when I left and not when I arrived. As far as the Vikings were concerned, this wasn't bad at all.

I could think of a few of my last voyages that landing at when I left might not be the safest place to be. Just saying.

We were still plastered together for a few seconds after successfully jumping, with me holding her around the waist like the cover of a scandalous science fiction book. "Hi," I told her, waggling my eyebrows. "What's a girl like you doing in a place like this?"

She pushed away from me. "What's the date?"

"It's January 17, 794 A.D. and we're on Svalbard, a lovely little mega island which is about halfway between Norway and the North Pole and is home to some of most merry band of Vikings that ever lived. In a few hundred more years from now people will refer to this little patch of frozen heaven as part of the Arctic. Also, the summer is around forty-three degrees, tops," I peered around at the barren snow-covered, mountainous island. "History says that the Vikings didn't discover this place until the twelfth century."

It was around 10:00 in the morning and the wind was blowing like it always did. It really was a beautiful place. The sunshine reflecting off the snow was blinding and we both squinted hard against glare for a bit until we got used to it. We were at the bottom of a valley a few miles outside of the village I had hung with for over three months. The trees were thick but bare, giving us a pretty good view of our surroundings.

Then it started snowing. Not heavy, just steady.

Pointing, I said, "Nearest settlement is that way. I stayed with these folks a while so I'm kind of a local celebrity."

"How long, exactly?" Chloe asked as she fell in step behind me, trudging through the snow.

"A tad over three months."

"You've got to be kidding me."

"Nope," I told her. "If I recall, finals were due and I wasn't ready for all the paperwork, so I decided to take a few months off."

"I do suppose that you being friends with anyone we come in contact with is a plus," she admitted.

The snow had started picking up after we'd walked about five minutes, clinging to our overcoats while we traversed through the bare trees in the direction that I was hoping would lead us to the village. "How much time do we have here?" Chloe asked suddenly.

"Huh?"

"On the glove. Doesn't it tell how long until the next jump?"

Oh. I hadn't thought of that. Checking the glove, I found that we had almost six hours to burn. Which was fine by me because I was really looking forward to the hospitality of my Viking brethren. "Right at six hours," I said. "Good. Wait until you taste some of the food around here. It's divine."

"I'm sure," Chloe said, sighing.

I glanced back at her. "No, really, it is," I started to say, but the arrow burying into the tree a foot away from my head made me stop talking.

"Get down!" I shouted, grabbing Chloe's shoulder and pulling her to the ground with me. Then, to whoever was using us as target practice, I called, "It's Jericho."

Silence. Then I heard scuffling in the distance as someone came out in the open with a drawn bow and nocked arrow. With relief, I saw that I knew the archer.

"Piper, you're a sight for sore eyes, let me tell you," I said, smiling broadly.

"Jericho?" Piper said, confusion evident on her face before she smiled back. I guess to her I'd only been gone maybe an hour. "Why are you still here? You said you wouldn't be back for a long time when you left," she told me, trotting the short distance between us and grabbing me in a big hug.

"I'm glad you're back," she said, her voice small and sincere. "Something's happened."

I pulled away, holding her shoulders and looking at her. "What?"

"The pact with the southern war-bands is no more," Piper said.

I frowned. "I know. That happened about a week ago. I thought you said everything would be fine when Bjourn went to talk to them."

Piper didn't say anything, but her face sure did.

"Where's Bjourn?" I asked her, trying not to sound harsh or rushing. The problem is that when I was here last, I'd told Bjourn the Berserker not to try and meet with the south yet.

But you know Vikings. Stubborn isn't a strong enough word.

"They've taken him," she said, her face saddening.

I dropped my hands from her shoulders, growled in frustration, kicked a small bush and ended my tantrum with my hands on my hips and pacing in the snow.

"I told him," I said, shaking my head. "But no, not Bjourn the flipping Berserker. No way was he going to let this thing go and ruin his street cred."

Okay, for those of you who're a little lost as to what was exactly going down right at that moment, I'll sum it up for you.

I'd been hunting, fishing, skinning, and hunting some more with Piper and her entourage for two months, and also, at the request of Bjourn and his brother Bulwark the Mighty, had been sitting in on the lovely little war councils they had every Thursday night at around 6:00. Well, it really started at 6:30 but we all liked to get there early to catch up with each other and drink honey mead until it actually started.

I never found out why they referred to it as a war council considering there wasn't a war going on.

Anyway, in one of the later meetings, a ragged scout had brought news that Bjourn's southern borders, which were off limits by the war-bands on the opposite side of it, were being patrolled daily by the southern tribes.

Being the brilliant diplomat that I am, I told Bjourn that, even though they weren't actually breaking any rules by just riding the fence line, so to speak, he probably should get in touch with them and see how relations were. Since shooting someone an email wasn't an option in 793 A.D., people often made pacts and didn't speak to each other for years.

Since I could be away from danger anytime I wanted in less than ten seconds, I even offered to go as his emissary. Long story short, Bjourn told me no, called the scout a craven, then motioned for a serving girl to refill his mead horn.

Two weeks later, the southern war-bands sent word that the pact was no more by attacking one of Bjourn's hunting parties, resulting in two casualties and several wounded hunters. Bjourn then bellowed about the outrage and decided that he was going to have a chat with them. I told him not to and that it was the worst idea in the history of worse ideas, to no avail.

So he left.

And a few days later, so did I, telling Piper, whom I spent most of my time with, that I wouldn't be back for a long time.

So there I was, back in an hour or so and hearing that Bjourn the Berserker, leader and ruler of the northern war-bands, didn't listen to me and got himself captured. Funny how so much could change in sixty minutes.

"You weren't hunting, were you?" I told Piper, looking her

up and down and noticing the extra armor and lack of dead animals slung at her side. She always was a good shot.

"Scouting," she said. "We heard that southern forces were marching our hills, so Bulwark sent me."

"Where is Bulwark?" I asked.

"In council at the moment." Piper said, looking embarrassed and adding, "Sorry for letting that arrow loose."

Then Piper finally noticed Chloe, the girl standing a few feet away watching our exchange. "Who's she?" she asked, looking Chloe up and down. "And what are you two wearing?"

"The clothes are a long story," I said, looking at Chloe, who happened to be glaring at Piper. Obviously she wasn't too thrilled about the way Piper was looking at her. "And this is Chloe, a friend of mine. Chloe, meet Piper."

Chloe offered her hand and Piper shook it. "Well met, stranger," she said.

"Charmed," Chloe said, her voice dripping with tons of, I don't know, something that I didn't like. At least she knew the language, I guess.

"Piper, why don't you take point? We'll see you back at the village in a few minutes," I told her, never taking my eyes off my embarrassing Russian comrade.

"Just be careful, Jericho," Piper said, touching my shoulder one last time before jogging into the snow-laden forest.

"What the heck was that?" I shot at Chloe once I was sure Piper was out of earshot.

"What was what?" Chloe asked innocently.

"You know what I mean, Chloe."

Clearly it was time to let my traveling companion know a few things about time-travel etiquette.

"Her village is in shambles because their leader has been taken captive by a band of invading enemies bent on her and her people's destruction and you decide that sarcastic disdain is the best way to say hi?"

Trying, and failing, to rival my vehemence, she said, "She was looking at me like—"

"Like what?" I asked sharply, cutting her off. "Like someone she didn't know while scouting her forest for possible enemies? While you were acting like a high-school cheerleader checking out competition, she was genuinely wondering where the Helheim you came from, and with good reason."

Chloe just stared at me, not knowing what to say.

"I know you think we're just here for six hours, and we are, but these are all real people with real problems and real swords pointed at them. You're not just watching a movie that'll be over soon and you can get on with your life. You're really here, right now."

And with that, I turned and started for the village without another word. I did stop to make sure Chloe was following me, only she wasn't.

"Well, come on, sunshine, we don't have all day."

I was still mad while we trekked through the snow out of the forest and into the field where I'd snapped pictures of Piper doing a headstand, then a few of her fishing, then a few of her smiling at me. It seemed so long ago, but in reality, for me, it'd only been about two weeks.

Then a spear stuck in the dirt a few inches from my right foot.

I'm going to go with my being so irate at Chloe that I wasn't paying attention to the band of marauding warriors bearing down on us, riding some of the largest horses imaginable.

I'm not really a quick thinker most of the time. Just being honest. My body has been classically conditioned over many years to wince upon hearing the words "think fast" since I was always hit with something after they were uttered.

But when presented with life-threatening situations, like being attacked by a raiding band, I'm actually not that bad. The old fight or flight kicked in pretty quick.

Snatching up the spear in my gauntlet clad right hand, I rushed at the three men on heavy horses, reared back, hopped one step, and launched it at them. The man I'd been aiming for must've also been one of those guys who got hit when presented with a think fast maneuver, because I got him in the left shoulder, de-horsing him.

"Get away!" I shouted at Chloe, a pointless gesture considering she'd already bolted at the nearest warrior and somehow vaulted onto the back of his horse, surprising me and especially the rider. Well, I mean, I know that I would've been surprised if some chick in a Nazi coat jumped on the back of my horse. Since the dude's face was shadowed by the heavy helm he was sporting, the only inclination I had of his surprise was when he screamed and tried to throw a few elbows at his new riding partner.

I also saw that the dude turned out to be a dudette. Which was a real bust because I was too busy trying not to die to be able to enjoy the medieval girl-fight that ensued once the both of them hit the ground and started rolling around in a tussle.

Let me pause here a moment to tell you, whoever-you-are, that normal soldiers, after receiving a spear in the shoulder, would be out for the count or, at the very least, retreating.

But Vikings are not your normal soldiers.

The guy I hit was the first one to me, slashing at me with his huge great sword, which he was using in one hand, not the easiest thing to do considering how much one of those things weigh. I rolled to my left, managing to get my body out of the way of the wide blade but not my long coat, which, after my bout with the wounded warrior, wasn't long anymore.

I didn't have time to congratulate myself on yet another survival because the second man, who was brandishing a spear, tried to take a stab at me. Catching the weapon just below the spearhead, I gave it a hard tug as he rode past, completely pulling him off his horse.

"If you weren't so stubborn," I said, planting a foot on his armored chest and wrenching the spear from his hand, "you'd learn to let go." Whirling around, I ran at the first attacker, who still had the spear lodged in his shoulder. But just as I reared back to sail my second spear at him, an arrow buried in his throat.

Ouch. A spear was one thing, but something told me he wasn't about to just walk that one off.

But you know what? The dude kept coming at me, his sword held high for an attack.

"What the heck, dude?" I shouted, taking a stance with my spear. I was glad when he fell almost ten feet from me. It would've been a little embarrassing to maybe die at the hands of a man about to be dead himself.

"Be careful, Jericho," Piper said, stepping to my right.

"Yeah, no kidding," I muttered.

"Jericho!" I heard Chloe scream. Spinning on my heel I saw that the warrior woman she'd tried to take down didn't exactly want to go down without a fight, if Chloe being swung hard by her arm and doing a face plant in the snow was anything to go by.

"Piper," I said, pointing at the woman who had produced a dagger and was about to pounce on Chloe with it.

Piper nocked another arrow into her bow and sent it sailing. Her arrow struck true, burying into the warrior chick's left leg. This slowed her down, but she still limped another few feet, grabbed Chloe out of the snow, and put the dagger to her throat while using her as a body shield.

Piper pulled another arrow and was about to draw when I placed a hand on her bow, "Don't do it, Pipe. I know you're good, but she can't die."

"Get my horse," said the warrior woman that held Chloe captive. "You, with the glove."

I held up my hands. "Look, lady, we've all had a doozy of a day so far. Why don't you just put the dagger down?"

"My horse," she growled again, taking a step back and dragging Chloe with her. I saw the blade bite into skin and saw blood.

"Alright," I told her, starting in the direction of the warhorse almost thirty feet away. "Just take it easy."

Once I'd snagged the reins of the semi-skittish horse, I started toward the parley. Well, I mean, I thought it was going to be a parley, anyway. You know, switch Chloe for the horse. But once I was standing ten feet away, the warrior woman made it clear that the one holding the hostage is the one who makes the rules.

She clicked her tongue and the horse started toward her. When it arrived, and don't ask me how because the stupid goliath of a horse was in the way, she somehow climbed into her saddle in two steps and, get this, dragged Chloe onto the horse with her.

Before I knew it, the warrior chick had kicked her horse into gear and was bounding away with little Chloe lying across her saddle with a knife to the back of her neck.

It took a few seconds for me to realize what had just happened, when I saw Chloe's glove slip from her hand during the tussle and land in the snow.

"Really?" I shouted, whirling to Piper. "Shoot her."

"I could hit your friend," she said, but I noticed she drew her arrow back.

"Try and hit her horse, or something," I said, waving at the quickly decreasing target like a maniac.

You know, Arabians once believed horses to be sacred animals. They treated them with the utmost respect, let them stay in their houses, bathe them twice a day and some even pray to them.

Piper wasn't an Arab. She happened to be a Viking. And Vikings, if you didn't know, eat their horses.

The first arrow missed by a few feet and my practically jumping up and down like a numbskull probably didn't help her shot because the second arrow missed, too, and by that time Chloe and her captor were too far away.

Just wow. I'd been there for, like, literally twenty minutes and I'd already lost Chloe to enemy Viking raiders.

Things weren't exactly looking good for the home team.

Chapter 23

Piper was a pretty levelheaded girl for a nineteen-year-old. Considering how girls her age acted in my time versus how she had to act just to not die on a daily basis really helped the nature versus nurture thesis I'd been working on. So when I lost it and started kicking snow into the air and growling like a pit bull on steroids she just stood there, her bow in hand.

Luckily, this only went on for about a minute, at which point I calmed down and felt foolish. "Where did they take her?"

"They have a lot of camps, Jericho," she said, slinging her bow across her back. Pointing in the direction Chloe had been dragged away, Piper added, "But since they went west, they could only be headed to one of two camps that way."

I perked up at that. "Really?"

Piper nodded. "Yes, but neither will be easy to get into with our heads still sitting on our shoulders."

Checking my gauntlet, I saw that I had five and a half hours left till the next jump. It just didn't look like enough time. Remembering Chloe's glove, I went to retrieve it. "How long will it take to get to either one of these camps?" I asked, bending over to pick the gauntlet up out of the snow.

"About five hours."

I stopped dusting the snow off the gauntlet and looked at her. "Seriously?"

She nodded, a small frown on her lips. "But longer if we can get Bulwark and his men to help us."

I was already shaking my head. "No, Piper, you don't understand. Five hours is already not enough time as it is."

"They aren't going to kill her. Most likely they'll put her to work or, if she's pretty enough, make her their chief's woman," Piper said, and I guess she was trying to help calm me down by telling me that.

I took a deep breath. How was I going to explain everything to her? I mean, I could rattle off the predicament in about ten seconds, but if she didn't understand it wouldn't help matters. The only thing I had to my aide was a fishing trip Piper and I had gone on alone that lasted about three weeks. I'd told more things to her than the rest of her brethren one night while we were curled up by a fire, huddled close so we didn't freeze to death.

I know. Romantic.

"Do you remember when I told you where I was really from?"

"You said you were from a different time. That was all."

The way she'd replied so quickly led me to believe that she'd thought about the conversation more than once. "I wanted to ask you more," she started, her voice trailing off as she looked anywhere but at me, her cheeks red.

It was a good fishing trip but un-flipping-believably cold.

"It's flipping f-freezing," I had said through chattering teeth while jumping up and down behind Piper, who was busy lighting a fire.

"You always sa-say th-that," she said, not in the least bit cold but mocking me with a beautiful smile on her face. "Don't be a baby. You'll be warm soon enough."

"I'm not so sure," I said, wrapping my arms tight around myself. "There's probably not enough fire in Helheim to warm me up right about now."

In a few minutes, though, Piper had a fire going with a few of our catch of the day thrust on sticks above it while we sat a few feet away curled up in what they called a fishing/hunting blanket. Not exactly like that because they called it either one depending on whether or not they happened to be fishing or hunting in the frigid weather. Since we were on a long fishing trip, the polar bear skin was called a fishing blanket that night.

And, dude, but it was a cozy skin. I actually had thought about bringing one back with me but decided against it considering the Vikings, unlike me, didn't have animal rights

people at every
street corner.

Probably a good thing, too, because after my three-month voyage of Vikingness, I now know why the polar bears are endangered. And if you're wondering whether or not I killed one while I was there—

No comment.

Where was I?

Oh yeah. Me and the beautiful warrior Viking girl cuddled up in bear skins in the middle of nowhere. Well, we weren't exactly cuddled together because, I don't know if you guys have ever had the chance to sit wrapped up in a polar bear skin, unlikely because of the you-know-who people, but those things are huge. So when I say Piper and I were sharing a blanket and you get all giggly and stuff, just let it be known that we might as well have been sharing a circus tent, because we had about that much space in our bear skin.

"You've got a good spear arm," Chloe said as she checked the fish with a knife.

Considering we had just been talking about what we'd done that day, I shrugged it off and smiled, saying, "Thanks, Pipe. Since you taught me I guess I should say that you do, too."

"Almost done," she said, sitting back and looking at the bear skin floor. I could sense that she was purposely not looking at me and I took the moment to examine her white-blonde hair, noticing the dark spots from the melted snow.

Then, for some crazy reason, I blurted, with my arms wrapped around my knees drawn to my chest, "I'm not from here, Piper. I'm from another time."

When I say crazy reason, I mean because I really thought the world of Piper, realized it as she shyly complimented my spear arm and looked at the ground and decided that I wanted to be honest with her. So, yeah, that was my crazy reason.

"I really like you, you know," she said, her eyes still on the skin covered ground. "I don't know when you plan on leaving but I'd rather you stay if you can or take me with you if you can't."

This was a lot for Piper, who wasn't much on talking. I'd been with them almost three months and she wanted to leave with me. Most guys would think this a real score.

I was thinking this was exactly what I was hoping Piper wouldn't say. I'd seen her looks at times, felt her gaze, heard the jokes her friends made to her about me, but I thought I'd be gone before she got the courage to tell me anything like what she was telling me right then.

What was I supposed to say? Did I like her back? Well, duh, I mean, I was currently on a three-week fishing trip with just her. Clearly I liked her company, but was that all? Did I just like being around her and causing her to blush and smile with my signature charm and wit?

Or did I really like Piper, the Viking warrior chick from 794 A.D.?

"Piper, I think you're great. But I can't take you with me when I leave," I said after an awkward pause.

See? That sentence didn't say whether or not I did or didn't like her.

"Why?" Piper asked, looking up at me. Sometimes in my time-traveling I'm presented with a situation that makes me think, "What the heck, Jericho? What're you doing, man?"

Piper's heart-wrenching look was one of those times.

"Because I have...duties," I tried.

"Like what? I could help," she said hopefully, causing me to feel like a cad even though I hadn't done anything.

"Not with these kind of duties, Piper," I said. "I'm a teacher of sorts where I come from and also a soothsayer/seer/know-it-all and in severely high demand."

Piper looked at me a few more seconds, making me feel dreadful, before simply nodding, checking the fish one last time, and saying, "Food's done."

And that was pretty much it. The trip lasted another two days and we went back to the village. I was there a few more days and left.

To say that I hadn't thought of Piper at all when I went home would be a lie. I had thought of her and about what she'd told me. I had also been rehearsing what I would tell her when I saw her again because I was definitely going back one day.

But right then, after Chloe had been abducted and I was trying to explain to Piper why I needed to ride like the wind after her, I still didn't know what to say.

"It's fine," I told her. "I wasn't exactly my smoothest that night."

"What about where you're from?" Piper asked, changing the subject.

"I'm from the future," I said simply.

Pulling her eyebrows down in thought she asked, "How far in the future?"

"Well, it's 794 now," I said. "And I'm from 2012 so twelve-hundred and eighteen exactly."

Piper was staring at me like I'd just told her I was a girl. "You're serious?"

Nodding, I said, "Look, I know it's a lot to take in but it's true."

"So you can just go anywhere, anytime you choose? How?"

Tapping my gauntlet, I told her, "My gauntlet. This is what takes me to any time I want," I decided that explaining the mechanics of it and where it had come from wasn't exactly important right then, so I left that out. "But here's my dilemma, Piper, I can't control where or when I'm going for a while and it's saying that I only have a little over five hours left here before it takes me somewhere else and if Chloe's not here with me when that happens, she'll be left and probably never see her father again."

Piper's brows were still furrowed, but I could see she was starting to catch on. "So it's broken."

I was taken aback. "What? No," but then I thought of the fact that it was basically taking me on joyrides that I wasn't exactly digging and, to be honest, that didn't sound fixed to me. So thanks for nothing, Dr. Atrium Sparks.

"Essentially, yeah, I guess it is broken," I said. "Now do you see why I have to go after Chloe now?"

Without another word about my when, where, what, who, or why, Piper started walking. "We'll need horses."

"That's my girl," I told her, falling in step behind her as we trotted toward her village.

This wasn't going to be easy or fun, I knew it. But I was really glad Piper was helping me because right then, in the snowy mountains of Svalbard, she was my only hope.

Or, more specifically, Chloe's only hope.

Chapter 24

Piper's home town looked pretty much the way I'd left it. Cold, damp, cheery and a tad drunk on ale.

"Jericho, my friend," a blacksmith by the name of Olger said to me, smiling broadly and clapping me on the shoulder, "I didn't expect to see you back so soon."

Olger was the one who'd made the cool double-bladed battle-axe for me and was a great guy. "I forgot a friend of mine who happened to be kidnapped by your enemies, Olg, nothing more."

Nodding knowingly, like kidnapped friends were the absolute norm on Svalbard, Olger said, with a friendly hand on my shoulder, "Aye. Had a friend kidnapped by the southern tribes once."

"Really? What happened?"

Shrugging, the blacksmith said, "Never saw him again. Heard he was flayed from neck to belly and mounted on stakes."

Piper must've seen the look on my face at the mentioning of flaying and staking because she cut our village visit down to a few minutes. Bulwark the Mighty wasn't too keen on Piper escorting me behind enemy lines but, because he and I were old chums who used to sit beside one another on the Thursday night war council meetings, he let us go.

Actually, I might've thought I was losing him and decided to throw in that we'd also look around for any signs of his older brother while we were around the enemy camps, which was probably the only reason he said yes. He also insisted, since I had somehow lost my weapons I'd had not an hour ago when I left, that I take his weapons.

"No thanks, Bulwark," I told him. "I don't plan on coming back afterwards and I'd hate for Piper to have to tote all of your stuff back. This is just a pit stop."

After I'd acquired a two-handed great-sword slung on my back with a bow and quiver, I was ready to go. Piper was what the Vikings called a shield-maiden, which meant she used one-handed weapons and a shield. I'd already found out she could use any weapon she felt like using but just preferred the sword and shield.

In exactly two minutes we were standing next to our mounts, fully equipped for our journey. Since I was trying to hurry, I didn't take the time to garb myself from head to toe in Viking clothes, which I hated to not do because they were so comfortable. I did lose my Nazi long coat, though, exchanging it for a small form-fitting sleeved coat of mail and a few wolf skins around it.

Also, and this isn't for all ears, finding a coat of mail small enough to fit me was almost impossible, so I ended up borrowing it from Piper.

What? It's flipping chain, whoever-you-are, which is completely unisex, and it went great with my black Chuck Taylors. What can I say, black goes great with pretty much everything.

I stepped up into the saddle of my black and white war horse and checked my glove. Four hours and fifty minutes left. "You ready, dear?" I asked Piper as she climbed into her saddle.

"I was going to ask you that," she told me, causing me to frown because Chloe had said the exact same thing to me once.

My reply was a heel to my horse. "Later, guys," I called over my shoulder. "I'll be back one day. You guys rock."

So with that, the two of us, aided by the cheers of our Viking comrades at our backs, left the village and went in search for the helpless Russian girl from 2340.

We hit the snow-covered ground hard, turning our mounts west and kicking them into high gear. They just don't make horses like they used to, is all I'm going to say. Your average 2012 steed wouldn't have made it thirty minutes at our punishing pace, let alone the two and a half hours the Viking mounts accomplished. We stopped by an icy creek, dismounting and leading the lathered beasts to it and letting them get a good drink.

"How much further?" I asked, checking my gauntlet. "Because my legs are killing me."

"Another hour to the first camp," Piper said, patting the neck of her tired horse. "The next one is another half hour or so from that one, but the good thing is we'll know whether or not your friend is in either one of them from a distance if our timing is right."

I didn't like the sound of that at all. "Let's get moving," I said, pulling the reins of my horse in mid-drink.

"They need more time, Jericho."

"Well, what do you know, so do I."

Piper stepped in front of me, putting her hands on my chest softly yet with some firmness. "If you kill or lame the horses, you surely will not have the time you so desperately need."

We stood there for what seemed like a long time with our eyes locked while my poor horse was pulling at his reins trying to get at the water again.

Not knowing what came over me, I let go of the reins. "Come here," was all I said, pulling her into a hug. She didn't resist at all and wrapped her arms around my waist, placing the side of her head on my mailed chest. It wasn't the most amorous of hugs, but it was sincere.

"You're doing a lot for me, here," I said and felt her melt into me.

"I don't even know who she is," she finally said.

"She's a Russian girl from the year 2340 with some anger issues," I said. "Her father made the gauntlet and he's in danger right now and we're the only people who can help him. Keeping Chloe alive is one of my top priorities at the moment."

Piper pulled away a little and looked me in the face again, placing a cold hand on my cheek. "How is this any of your responsibility? How can anyone from any time other than your own be any reason to risk your life? Even me. What am I to you?"

The question wasn't a hard one. "You're my friend," I told her. "So are the rest of your brethren. So is Chloe."

Wow. Did I really just friend-zone a gorgeous Viking warrior woman?

"Just a friend?" Piper asked, one side of her mouth lifting into a smile while her index finger did something to my sideburn that felt great and made me want to close my eyes and go to sleep.

I reached up and covered her hand with mine. "That's all I got right now, Piper. But, I have to say, I do so love this little island of yours."

"Thanks. Made it myself," she said, smiling.

"Shut up," I told her, shoving her away and laughing. "Look at us laughing in the face of danger like a couple of champs."

It really was crazy. More so after we waited till I had two hours left on my clock before mounting up again on our halfway refreshed horses. We rode in silence for what seemed like fifty-three minutes because, well, that's exactly how long we'd been riding in silence before Piper, who was in the lead, held up a hand and we stopped in a small outcrop of trees.

"How much longer do you have?" she asked, dismounting.

"Hour and seven minutes," I told her, dropping off my horse and into the ankle-deep snow, instantly hating my choice of not changing out my shoes for Viking ones.

"Not too bad," Piper stated, pulling off her bow. "Better make it count, though."

We tied the horses to a few smaller trees and exited the outcropping and in less than a minute we could see the first enemy village better. Piper crouched down at the top of a hill that overlooked the rather small and surprisingly quiet village.

"She's not here."

"How do you know?" I asked, squatting beside her.

"It's a gift. She's not here," she said simply, standing. "We need to hurry. If Chloe's captor didn't stop here, then we might catch her before she makes it to the other village."

After we made it back and exited the small section of trees on our horses, I asked, "What do you mean it's a gift?"

Reaching a hand to her neck, Piper pulled down her snow-fox pelt, exposing her right collarbone and the horrific burn on it. "The southern war-bands have a way of welcoming women captives into their camps."

My mouth was hanging open for a while before I regained enough composure to ask, "When did it happen?"

"When I was twelve. A lot of us were taken during the border wars back then," she said casually, like she was talking about how deep the snow got at this time of year. "Since I was so young, they put me to work in their meat huts and tending to the sheep. Some of the older women weren't so lucky. They're very ceremonial and loud about...She's not here."

I was starting to catch on to what she was saying, and I was also starting to feel sick. Geez, but could this day get any worse?

Then my horse tripped in a hole and broke its right front leg.

So, yeah, I suppose the day could and did get worse.

Since I was so high off the ground on the mountainous beast, I was somehow flung forward and ended up with a mouthful of snow instead of being crushed by my ride.

"Are you hurt?" Piper asked urgently, stopping her horse beside me as I got to my knees and started trying to knock snow off.

"I'm not dead," I confirmed. By this time my horse was making the most pathetic of noises that grated on my ears. Standing, I started for it, pulling the great-sword off my back. "Sorry, pal," I said, and meant it. "I'll never forget you, homie."

Then I finished the job.

You know how I said once that blood and sand mix a little too well? Well, blood and snow is way worse. Mainly because it looks like a strawberry daiquiri snow-cone.

"Let's go," I said, accepting Piper's hand and climbing up behind her. In spite of all the unfortunate events that had taken place in the last few hours, I still was able to somehow say, while I adjusted in my seat and wrapped my arms around Piper's waist, "Man, you smell good."

Laughing, Piper kicked our last hope and we were off.

And she did smell good. Kind of like an earthy, warm yet cool scent that a guy could get lost in. The wonderful smelling ride lasted another half hour or so and I really must've been lost in the scent, or something, because I didn't look at my gauntlet until we stopped a little outside of the village.

Nineteen minutes left and counting.

"Okay, so what's the plan here?" I asked after we'd both dismounted and started for the seriously loud town. And when I say loud, I mean, like, really loud. It sounded like the Super Bowl of the Vikings.

Ha. Like the *Vikings* will ever get to the Super Bowl.

See what I did there?

"Get inside and find your friend."

"Don't forget to do it in less than eighteen minutes, also," I threw in.

Close to the town I produced Chloe's gauntlet she'd dropped and put it on my left hand. This had been an idea of mine since I'd first met Chloe in Rome and saw that she was sporting a left-handed glove. "Never done this before," I said.

Piper frowned in confusion while I turned and aimed both hands at nothing in particular, firing off two bolts of white-blue electricity that reached almost fifty yards. I smiled broadly and looked at my hands, the bright lights in the palms of both gauntlets fading slowly and made me feel like a lightning mage.

Fan-flipping-tastic.

A crude, sorry excuse for a town gate was standing wide open when we entered quietly, except I'm not sure why we were sneaking due to the racket the town's occupants were making. "What're they doing?" I asked nervously, following Piper through the empty streets.

"Branding captives is kind of like their entertainment," Piper said.

Then we made it to the town square with fourteen minutes left.

Wait. Is it making you nervous with me letting you know every time a minute or two ticked by without us being even close to saving Chloe?

Well, good. Imagine how I felt right about then, whoever-you-are.

The square was packed to overflowing with Vikings who were all cheering and looking toward the center, which is where I spotted Chloe. She seemed to be doing a lot better than you'd expect a captive to be doing. I mean, she was still wearing all her clothes, her lip wasn't bleeding, her eyes weren't blacked, and she seemed to have all her body parts. She didn't look like she was having the most grand of times, though, if the horrified expression on her face was anything to go by.

Two armed guards stood on either side of Chloe, escorting her to the center of the screaming mob and onto what looked like gallows, which made me gasp, except that it was missing the whole gallow part of gallows that make them all, you know, gallowy.

So it was basically a stage.

Checking my right gauntlet, I saw that I had twelve minutes left. I had no plan. I mean, there was always the old snatch and grab maneuver, but with a load of screaming Vikings crammed into a town square to stop me, I was thinking that the odds of landing that trick were slim.

Except that none of the screaming Vikings had handfuls of lightning like yours truly.

"Alright, Pipe, here's the deal," I started, explaining my outrageous plan to save Chloe, who had just been forced to her knees by the two guards.

Eleven minutes.

Screaming to try and get attention away from Chloe and on me was impossible due to the abundance of screaming already going on, so I decided to jolt them another way.

Ha.

When I was six a couple of schoolmates of mine and I liked to play with a farmer's electric fence by one of us grabbing it and then making a chain of bodies so we'd all get a little of the juice.

A version of that grade school fun happened when I shot my bolts of lightning into the crowd on my left, only it was about fifty bajillion times worse.

If you're worried about the children don't you worry your pretty little head about that, whoever-you-are.

Because I got them, too.

I wasn't exactly able to pick my targets and it wasn't like I killed anyone. I just hurt them really, really, really, really, *really*, bad. The demented offspring of these violent warmongers wasn't exactly something I was worried about at the time.

I made a mad dash through the disoriented and hurting crowd toward the stage Chloe was on. "Chloe!" I yelled at her, waving my arms like a madman.

I wasn't really trying to cue her to do anything. Honestly, I was just trying to let her know that Jericho Johnson was on the case and that everything was under control, but then someone grabbed me from behind and threw me down, commencing to plant several hard stomps to my back and shoulders. I think it was the third time my face smashed on the ground that my eyes caught sight of my glove.

Ten minutes.

Before whoever was tap dancing on me could finish his painful performance, I rolled to my right and saw that my attacker happened to be the very woman who'd taken Chloe captive. She didn't look too surprised, so I was thinking she'd been expecting me. Since I wasn't feeling like Maximus the Merciful, I let loose two bolts from both hands at the poor chick standing not three feet away, sending her flying through the air and landing in a shaking heap almost fifteen feet away.

I kicked back onto my feet, which was one of the first things Evonne had taught me to do, and looked around for Chloe in the crazy town square. People were running away and screaming like Odin himself had shown up with a vengeful vehemence against them.

I couldn't see her and started panicking. Where had she gone? She had been right on the stage and then, *poof*, she'd vanished. I ran to the stage and up the stairs, scanning the wild crowd for any sign of Chloe.

"Ah, come on," I said.

Then I saw her being dragged away by her two guards on the other side of the square. Well, they were dragging her until one of them got an arrow in his back from Piper, who I had told to get on the nearest roof she could and provide cover fire. She seemed to be doing a bang up job of it.

All Chloe needed was for one of the guards to let go of her and she went to work. With her hands bound and ankles shackled together, Chloe jumped into the air and planted both of her feet into the remaining guard's chest, sending him sailing into a rock wall. I leaped from the stage and ran toward her, jolting anyone who got in my way as I traversed the maddening street.

"Did you really think I'd let you out of our date that easily?" I asked Chloe, skidding to a stop beside her.

Chloe was breathing hard when she shrugged. "A girl has to keep trying."

"Yeah, well, stop," I said, cutting the ropes that held her hands like hot butter with the sharp point of one of the gauntlet fingers. "No chance of cutting through the shackles like that, huh?"

Before she could answer we saw several attackers rallying from both sides of us.

"Please tell me you're not out of ideas," Chloe said, examining the opposition.

"Not just yet," I said, grabbing her around the waist and firing off my grappling hook.

Okay, I'm going to stop here and explain the grappling hook mechanics so you don't get this whole Batman vibe from it.

Here's the thing: the anchor comes out of the palm of the glove from the same place the bolts of electricity come from after selecting it from the dropdown menu. It looked like a mini version of a claw game and clamps on or into anything it hits and then would let go without resistance once I got to it. It was also a tiny thing for something that is supposed to hold my weight while it zips me around on a wire that's so small it's almost not visible.

Let me also point out to all you gamers, fan boys, comic book junkies or anyone else with nerd-like tendencies that the grappling hooks you've read about, seen or used in a game aren't very realistic.

I mean, do you know how fast someone has to be pulled to maintain a diagonal line for almost thirty feet from the ground to a roof?

About a bone-shattering one-hundred and fifty miles per hour.

So when I say I used the grappling hook, don't get this mental picture of me zip lining around like a flipping comic book because I didn't.

My anchor sunk into a beam on the peak of the nearest roof and Chloe and I ran toward the wall as it began pulling us quickly. It wasn't the easiest thing I'd ever done, and quite frankly I'm not even sure how we managed to kind of run up the wall and to the top of the steep roof while we held onto each other the whole miraculous way.

However it was accomplished is irrelevant, considering we escaped a lot of angry Vikings in the process. I checked my gauntlet.

Six minutes.

"What now?" Chloe asked me.

I saw Piper a few roofs away and waved to her. Returning the wave, she started her descent to the ground. "Meet up with Piper and get the heck out of here is my plan. Unless you just want to stick around and see what happens when I'm gone in five minutes."

An arrow hit the beam we were straddling, and we glanced at the street to see a handful of the more not-so-conservative

Vikings had started sailing arrows at us. Chloe rolled to the other side, grabbing the beam and lying down on the steep roof.

I had other plans.

Standing, I held my hands almost a foot apart facing palms and shot my bolts into each other.

I'm not sure what I'd been expecting, and I'd probably watched way too much anime for my own good, but the results weren't too shabby, if I do say so myself.

When connected, the bolts formed together into a sort of ball. The only problem was, if you guys remember from the beginning of this tale, I could only hold a steady stream of the stuff for close to thirty seconds. I'm guessing that when combined into a potent ball of juice that time was reduced drastically because I began to feel warmth in my palms and I could've sworn I saw smoke. Then I tossed the ball back into the Vikings court.

Again, I didn't know what to expect from what was supposed to be my Hadouken-level, deal-breaking finishing move. I mean, what if it had hit the ground and did what most electricity does when grounded and fizzled out or something lame like that?

These were my thoughts as the lightning the size of a small beach ball landed amongst the attacking Vikings.

My next thoughts were that I hoped there weren't any kids down there because this time I did feel bad.

Chloe wasn't touched at all by the ramifications of my bolt-bomb, unlike me, who, after the explosion was blown off my feet, landing on my back on the steep roof. I would've slid off had Chloe not grabbed my ankle.

"Four minutes, woman," I shouted at her through all the noise of sheer pandemonium and loud crackles of electricity, "let's move."

It took too long to get outside the crazy town.

Two minutes.

"Never flipping again," I said loudly, limping quickly after Chloe and Piper. My ears were ringing and one was bleeding, and

I couldn't feel my back for some reason. I was guessing I wasn't paralyzed because I was, you know, running, but it still wasn't the best feeling. Then I ran into Piper because she'd stopped suddenly.

"What about Bjourn?" she asked, glancing back at the village we'd just exited, which now had large pillars of smoke billowing from it into the sky. I was about to tell her that he was out of luck when, you're not going to believe this because I was there and I still couldn't, Bjourn the Berserker, speaking of the devil, ran out of the town gates, his bound hands clutching a bloodied broadsword and his ankle shackles broken.

"There he is," I said, my head still ringing.

Ninety seconds.

"Jericho," Bjourn said, smiling broadly for a guy who'd been a prisoner for almost two weeks. "Back so soon?"

"I forgot a friend of mine," I said.

Like Olger had done, Bjourn nodded knowingly like what I'd just said was a very normal thing. "Well, thanks for the diversion. It was enough for me to make an escape."

I sliced his bonds and saw that I had one minute left. "No worries, friend. Try to not let the bards destroy my faithful deeds in wild verse, Bjourn," I said, smiling at him and extending a hand.

Shaking my gauntlet-clad hand, he placed a hand on my shoulder and assured me that while he still drew breath, he would not stand for any wild songs written by any bard.

Thirty seconds.

"There's a horse in the outcrop for you and Piper to make it back home with," I said, taking a step back. "Come on, Chloe. We still have to save the stupid world, I guess."

Piper stepped close and hugged me hard. "Thank you," she whispered.

Fifteen seconds.

"You're welcome, Piper. I'll be back one day," I said, pulling away and grabbing Chloe's hand. "Try and explain to Bjourn what's about to happen, would you?"

"Explain what?" Bjourn asked, frowning.

Ten seconds.

"Later, guys," I said, taking a few more steps away from them while holding Chloe's hand.

Then Bjourn received an arrow from behind, dropping him to his knees before he took two more in his back.

Five seconds.

Piper screamed and tried to catch him before his body hit the snow. Then I did the only thing I could do in the few fractured seconds I had left to help her. Just before the last second ticked away, I grabbed Piper with my free hand and pulled her hard away from Bjourn's body.

Then we were gone.

Chapter 25

Lossiemouth, Scotland, December 25, 1665

It was cold again on the shores of the humble fishing village of Lossiemouth, a quaint little town that I'd came to after first visiting Aviemore and Elgin further south. I was there to get more information about the War of the Scotts, a sort of family blood feud between a few brothers raised in the barony. I had stayed here for a while and ended my journey on the windswept shores of northern Scotland on Christmas day.

I remember leaving because it was a tad depressing.

Now I was back a few minutes after I'd left, and it was still depressing.

Piper ended up in a heap on the cold sand, crying while Chloe decided to, I don't know, check the perimeter, I guess, because she walked down the beach away from us.

I sat beside the bawling girl and pulled her up into a half sitting position, and that's how the first hour of my return to Scotland went. With Chloe standing a good distance away with her arms folded around herself for warmth, her captors had relieved her of her Nazi overcoat, and me with Piper's shaking head on my right shoulder and chest.

Thankfully, we only had about three hours to go before our next jump. Surely nothing too life-threatening could happen on the beach next to a rundown fishing village in the next three hours, right?

"Chloe, stay with Piper. I'm going into town to get us something to eat."

Without waiting for her to protest, I left them on the beach and entered the fishing village. It was exactly as I'd left it, which was a very good thing right about now. I entered the only tavern in the small town and headed for the bar. The shack looked like it had been burned once and the owners had tried to recover the burned places.

"Homer," I called, knocking on the bar. "Jericho's back. I forgot to grab some vittles for my journey."

Homer was a stoop-shouldered man in his late fifties and was a super nice guy. I'd spoken to him first when I arrived and we'd talked for a few hours. "Well, now, ye'r back," said the smiling man coming in through a side door and waddling behind the bar. "And ye'r after some wittles, ye say?"

"For me and my friends, if you'd be so kind."

Nodding, Homer said, "Aye, ye've got a mighty long journey before ye, Ah'd say. How many friends?"

"Three counting myself," I said, leaning on the bar and peering out the doorway that was lacking a door. "Been busy today?"

"Not really. 'Ad a few home folks in here earlier and some of the boys are swearin' that a ship is coming in," he frowned at me. "Are ye' wearin' bleedin' chain mail?"

"Long story," I told him, glancing back to the harbor. I didn't remember a ship from the beach. But I hadn't been exactly looking for one, either.

"Sure been cold, though," he said.

"A little, yeah."

"Might come a frost tonight."

"Really?"

"Yes, indeed."

"You guys don't associate much with the south, do you?" I asked.

"Not too much," Homer said as he put a jug of Scottish ale on the bar. "No cups so ye'll 'ave to share, Ah'm afraid."

"That's fine." I said then we heard shouting.

"It's a ship! I told you, lubbers," the voice of a boy called as he ran through the streets toward the shore.

Shaking his head while he placed a loaf of bread and wedge of cheese on the bar, Homer said, "Thinks 'e's a right pirate, that one. Nothing but trouble, if ye ask me."

I thanked Homer for the food and exited the shack,

heading back to the sea. Sure enough, the loud kid was right. A ship was pulling into the meager harbor. It wasn't a very big one, but still too big to actually use the dock and thus had to drop anchor over a-hundred yards out.

I found the girls just like I'd left them, except Piper had finished crying and was pacing while Chloe sat cross-legged on the sand and watched the ship lower longboats into the water.

"Here," I said, tearing off a hunk of bread and offering it to Chloe. "It's not Wendy's, but it'll stop the miss-meal cramps."

Chloe accepted the bread and took a small bite, chewed it up, swallowed it, then said, "I'm sorry about Svalbard."

She didn't need to say anything else. I knew that she was kind of a proud girl so that was all I needed. "Me, too," I told her before walking to Piper.

"How you doing?" I asked.

"I'm fine," she said quickly, then, "Where and when are we?"

Since it seemed she wasn't ready to talk about anything pertaining to her crying for over an hour, I accepted the change of subject. "Scotland around 1665. Also, Merry Christmas."

"What?"

Oh yeah. Vikings weren't exactly on the up and up with holidays other than their own. "Today is Christmas, a holiday where we give other people presents, receive them from other people, then watch the Charlie Brown special back home."

I actually have met Charles Schulz once. I really just wanted to confirm my suspicion that Linus was really the only true friend Charlie Brown had and that everyone else's friendship was based on his not screwing up, which, let's be honest, always happened to the poor guy. I was right, of course.

"Where is Scotland?" Piper asked, peering at the ship. "And why would someone sail the sea on such an unworthy vessel?"

I laughed. "Because they tried to recreate the Viking boats and couldn't," I told her, offering her some bread and cheese, which she took.

"Should we be worried about these people?" Chloe asked, walking over to us.

I shrugged. "I don't know. Far as I know ships don't come to port here, so I'm kind of curious who it even is. There's a lot of famous pirates around this time. Who knows, maybe we'll get lucky and meet one of them."

I was, of course, joking. I didn't have the notion of wanting to meet even the no-name pirates, much less the ones who were devious and violent enough to make a mark in history. The three of us ended up finding a large piece of driftwood to sit on while we watched the men in the boats row toward us.

We had about ninety minutes left on our clock when the first longboats pulled onto land and the occupants stepped out. They were an odd bunch, I'll tell you that much, and they didn't seem to be paying us that much attention except for the redheaded girl in a white flowing cotton shirt and brown pants who narrowed her eyes at us when she stepped onto the sand.

I waved at her with my gauntleted hand and smiled reassuringly at her to let her know we weren't any harm. I guess my smile wasn't reassuring enough because the girl approached us and asked, "Which way 'ter Aviemore, mate?"

"You're Scottish," I stated, noting her thick accent. "You tell me."

"Ah'm not in the mood, ye' lubber," she started but was cut off by the rather large man who came up behind her. "'Elp the men unload, Amelia. Ah'll talk to 'em."

The alleged Amelia left but not before glaring at me hard, to which I smiled and waved again. "Good to meet you, Amelia. Try and not kill anyone over there, okay?"

I don't know why I was being such a jerk. Maybe because madam fire-head wasn't exactly on her best behavior and I wasn't having a great day so far. I thought this more so when somehow, I wasn't sure how because she'd been standing over ten feet away, I was on my back in the sand, my legs on the log I'd just been sitting on, with Amelia straddling my chest and what looked like a movie prop samurai sword at my throat.

No one moved, which was great at the time because I didn't think this chick had taken her meds that morning and I wasn't sure just how far she was willing to go with her curved sword.

But just when you'd think I'd keep my mouth shut, I said, "Nice blade, carrots. Did you earn it or steal it?"

The look in her eyes told me I'd gone too far, but the big man ended up grabbing and dragging her off me. "Ah said 'elp the men, Amelia," he growled. "Just go, lass."

Amelia stomped off without glancing back this time.

I sat back down on the log between Piper and Chloe and rubbed at my neck. "She's a real charmer," I told the big man, who I just noticed was missing his left hand. "Something tells me her father is going to have a time marrying that piece of work off."

"Ah'm her father," he said.

"Oh," I said, stammering. "I mean, I wasn't implying—"

"Don't worry, lad. She only found out a few months ago."

"Oh, well, uh, congratulations, mister…?"

"Call me Stubbs."

"Alright, Stubbs," I said, jerking my chin at his shipmates. "Why are you guys headed to Aviemore?"

I wasn't sure that he'd heard me because he was frowning at the way we were all dressed. Then he said, while still frowning at our strange garb, "Ah'm from there. 'Aven't been back in a few years, though."

Piper and Chloe weren't exactly in the most talkative of moods and basically just sat like bumps on a log while I chatted with the one-handed man. "It's south. Just follow the road to Elgen and its a few days ride from there if you follow the river Spey."

Stubbs nodded once and extended a hand. "Thanks, mate. We'll leave you with it, then."

He turned and started walking away. "Hey, wait up," I called, jumping up and following him. "What's the name of your ship?"

"The *Starbuck* and it ain't my ship."

"Love the name," I said as I walked beside him toward the men unloading the longboats. "Who's the captain?"

"Bartolomew Português is his name," Stubbs told me. "Now if ye'll excuse me, sir, Ah best be 'elping the lads."

"Well met, Stubbs," I said, peering at the sailors.

"Likewise," he said and left me watching them.

"Hello, sir."

I turned to the voice and saw it was a guy about my age sporting a velvet purple long coat. "Hey, pal. What can I do for you?" I asked him, looking him up and down from his boots to his fiery red hair.

He glanced over his shoulders before leaning close to me and whispering, "You wouldn't by any chance happen to have a writing quill on you, would you, old chap?"

I frowned at the odd request and was about to tell him that I was fresh out of writing quills when the girl who'd tried to kill me saw our clandestine exchange and said, "Dinna' even think about it, Newton."

The red-haired man looked irritatingly at her before turning back to me and smiling hopefully.

"Uh, no. I'm fresh out of quills," I said, which caused a downcast sigh to escape the alleged Newton's lips.

Wait a second.

"Newton?" I asked. "Is that your name?"

The man rolled his eyes around in a sort of manner that had me thinking he was trying to remember his own name before saying simply, "Yes."

"Like, what's your full name?"

Not knowing why I was so interested in his full name, he frowned before telling me, "Isaac Newton."

Jackpot, baby.

"Don't move," I told him before racing back to where I'd left Chloe and Piper. Skidding to a stop, I dropped to my knees in front of them and grabbed each of their hands. "You're not going to believe who is standing not thirty feet behind me."

They exchanged glances before looking back at me. Chloe

shrugged while Piper asked, "Who?"

"Isaac flipping Newton!" I said, smiling like crazy. Then it hit me. "Wait. What the heck is he doing in Scotland in 1665? He's supposed to be home avoiding the bubonic plague and discovering gravity right now."

Wow. And today happened to be his birthday, too. What're the odds?

Standing, I left the baffled girls and walked back to Isaac Newton. "Say, man, just what're you doing here? I mean, you're supposed to be back home discovering—" then I thought of what would happen if someone gave him the name of his greatest discovery and finished with, "Discovering the, uh, many mysteries of the world and yet you're in Scotland with a band of pirates."

"We're buccaneers, friend," said a tallish man who appeared at my side. "I'm the captain of this merry band of men and unless you and your strange gloves have business with my friend here, then you best be on your way."

I held up my strange gloved hands and backed away. "Alright, fine. Don't tell me. See if I care. And try to do something nice for your friend here's birthday, would you?" I said as I turned away from them. "It's not every day a guy turns twenty-five, you know."

That was the bait wrapped around my intellectual hook.

"Wait," Newton called to me. "Stop, sir."

I stopped and waited for him to approach me. "How did you know it was my birthday?"

"Just a big fan," I said. "Look, you guys seem really busy, so I'll let you get back to it," I turned away again before remembering something. "Oh, and lay off the alchemy in another twenty years," then I turned away again before remembering one last thing. "And remember this more than anything, watch out for the flipping Exocoetidae book that'll be out in a few years because you might want to reserve a slot before that little jewel comes out. Anyway, peace," I said, smiling and leaving the dumbfounded pre-physicist blinking after me.

I guess I should've said spoiler alert first, but there you have it.

A detailed book about flying fish came out a few months before Isaac Newton's world-changing volume about gravity did and was so expensive that it almost caused the publishing of the most groundbreaking book ever released to not happen.

I sat beside the girls again and sighed. Then Chloe said, "I hope you didn't tell him too much."

Shaking my head, I said, "Nah. He's got too great of a life coming up for me to blurt it out."

"So why was he with them?" Piper asked.

I shrugged. "Not sure. But I think I might come back one day and find out. The worst part is that if I'd just hung around a few more minutes before leaving the first time I would've ran into them."

They both grunted in agreement and we all just sat in silence as the last of the pirates made it to shore, unloaded gear, and went into Lossiemouth. Checking my gauntlet, I saw we had twenty minutes left.

Here's to the most uneventful time-traveling jump ever.

We sat in silence for the remaining time on the blustering beach and just stared out at the sea. It was kind of peaceful, really, and I wasn't looking forward to the next jump. Although for some reason my gauntlet wasn't displaying where I was going next like it had in Dr. Sparks lab, I just couldn't think of any of the places I'd been that I would rather go to that was better than just sitting here doing nothing.

Five minutes left.

"Well, I guess we dodged a bullet here, kids," I said.

Then four men materialized almost twenty feet in front of me with their backs to us. Three of which were wearing battle armor.

"They're in Dragonovs," Chloe shouted, grabbing my arm and leaping to her feet. Then we were all running like crazy into the fishing town.

Something hissed from behind us and one of the

upcoming houses in our path exploded.

So much for the most uneventful time-traveling jump ever.

Me and my big mouth.

Chapter 26

"Split up and hide," I told the girls while we ran, not really sure where we were going. "Make them hunt for you."

"Be careful," Chloe said while Piper nodded, and they disappeared into the town, weaving between the old buildings. I was glad that they'd vanished so quickly, but I already knew where I was going.

"Get out, Homer," I shouted, bolting through his doorway. The bartender looked confused, so I decided that grabbing him and dragging him out was better than explaining the situation right then.

We were almost to the exit when one of the Dragonovs fired off another missile. I dropped to the floor when I heard the hissing sound, like a bottle-rocket going off, and pulled Homer down with me. The tiny missile miraculously entered through a hole in the wall, passed over our heads, then exited the hut through yet another hole.

Before I had the chance to tell Homer to thank his lucky stars that his shack was so crappy, the missile hit the very much sturdy house beside us, causing Homer's place to shudder. Grabbing his hand one more time, I monkey-crawled out the doorway as the roof caved in, pulling the older Scotsman behind me.

But I wasn't fast enough.

What was left of the ceiling collapsed and pinned Homer from the waist down in the rubble, causing him to cry out, pain evident on his lined face. I dropped to my knees beside him and started trying to pull up on the heavy wood on top of him. "Hang in there, Homer," I said between clenched teeth as I strained against the weight. "I'm going to get you out of here."

Something flashed in the corner of my eye and I turned my head just in time to see one of the hellish Dragonovs level his right arm down at us. "No," I shouted. "Wait!"

Then he fired off another missile toward the rubble. The explosion sent me skidding across the street. I groaned while my ears rang, and I couldn't hear anything but the accursed ringing when I climbed to my shaky feet and began staggering toward the flaming remains of Homer's shack. I started out on my feet but ended up crawling on my hands and knees because my head kept spinning and I felt like I was going to be sick. I found Homer about ten feet from his blown up hovel, on his back in the cold sand of the street staring up at the sky. He was missing a leg I saw as I crawled up to him and grabbed his hand. "Homer?"

"Ah never went 'ter sea like Ah wanted to," he gasped out and I could tell something other than his leg was damaged.

In movies and books when something like this happens and the guy holding the doomed man's hand says, "You're going to be alright," you know that he knows that the hurt person isn't, in fact, alright nor was he going to be.

I used to read or watch scenes like that and just shake my head and think the other guy was a huge liar to tell someone dying that.

But you know, in the real world, there really isn't anything else you can say besides that. But, since I'd taken several oaths to myself to never say that to someone dying, I ended up saying, "I'm so sorry, man."

"Dinna' worry, lad," he said, looking me in the eyes and squeezing my hand. "Maybe one day we'll meet again."

Then his hand slipped from mine and he was gone. I watched his face while what was left of his life drained away. Getting to a slumping position, I closed his eyes as I heard the unholy gyrating of gears and felt the presence of my attackers close behind me.

"Jericho Johnson?" someone asked in a normal voice and not one amplified or distorted by a battle-suit helmet.

Placing my hands on my thighs, I let my head roll back as I looked at the sky, sighed deeply, and then tried to get to my shaky feet. "Depends on who's asking," I countered, barely managing to regain my footing while turning to face them. "How'd you know my name?"

"I am Verde' von Klaus," the man about my height with a mustache said in a thick Russian accent. He also was sporting a gauntlet that looked to be a shiny black. "I was able to get a little information about you from Dr. Atrium before I came looking for you. It seems you happen to be in possession of my property."

"You don't say. Well, you just happened to kill a good friend of mine," I said, my voice quivering with rage. I let my eyes flick to my gauntlet, not wanting to think what he meant by getting a little information about me from Chloe's dad or how he did it. I only had two minutes left to find Chloe and Piper and get the Helheim out of here. But I was thinking Klaus didn't know that.

Klaus waved his hand like he was dismissing a child. "I care not for your friends."

I took a step toward him and all three Dragonovs held a loaded arm. "I'm guessing since you're probably a sadistic spawn of Satan that you never had a mother that taught you the courtesy of not killing random people to get what you want."

Klaus held up a hand and the Dragonovs lowered their arms. Then he walked the gap between us, stopped, and looked at both of the gauntlets I was wearing. "Why are there two of them?" he asked, frowning.

"Oh, you know," I said, "I loved the first one so much that I decided to grab another one while I was out picking apples."

"Give them to me," he said.

I had one minute left. Sixty seconds to save the day.

Now I had fifty-eight seconds because I just thought that.

Fifty-seven, fifty-six...

"Since you don't have a problem killing people, why don't you just have your goons shoot me? Because that's the only way you're getting these from me," I told him, hoping he'd say yes.

Not being one to dawdle it seemed, Klaus turned on his heel. "Have it your way," he said, standing behind his troops.

I'm guessing Dr. Sparks hadn't explained to Klaus

everything the gloves were capable of doing. I mean, if I had been him, there was no way I'd let some guy wearing not one but two flipping electrical conductors have a chance of firing on my men.

But that's just what he did.

Throwing up my hands before Klaus gave the order for them to kill me, I fired off both barrels, so to speak, hitting the Dragonovs who were, as luck would have it, standing close enough together to all share in the lightning fest.

Twenty seconds.

"Jericho!" I turned to see the girls rushing toward me.

"Come on," I shouted to them.

I held my streams till my gloves started to smoke and stopped. Klaus, who'd also been hit, was lying amongst his soldiers, his body jerking violently.

Ten seconds.

The last thing I saw of Klaus before we disappeared was his face as he tried to scream at us.

Then we were gone again to God knows where.

Looking back, I wish that I'd killed Klaus then and there. It would have solved a lot of problems and made this story a lot more enjoyable for me and everyone else in it. I keep telling myself that I didn't have the time to kill him and that if I'd tried, I might have left without Chloe or Piper.

But I should've taken that chance. Klaus needed to die then and there. Bottom line.

But he didn't. Which is why I can't completely tell you the end of this tale because, frankly, I'm not sure of the outcome myself. But there's still more to go.

Chapter 27

Dr. Cross pushed the stop button on the gauntlet's screen and the recorded voice ceased speaking. Leaning back in his desk chair, he removed his glasses and rubbed his eyes. Glasses weren't something you saw someone wear most of the time in 2342 because technology had ways of fixing flat eyes permanently in just a few minutes. But the rather young doctor had for some reason decided not to have the surgery done, to a lot of his staff's astonishment considering he was the one whose research in the field of human biology, anatomy, and nanotechnology had resulted in the most major breakthroughs in the last decade with eyesight, amongst other things people took for granted with age.

Pressing a button on his desk strewn with info-tabs, Dr. Cross asked the question he'd asked a few hours prior to his nurse, Ritu. "Is he still alive?"

He waited while Ritu, after a few seconds delay, like she was checking to make sure, walked into view, her green hologram face appearing as she answered, "Yes, but barely. His body is rejecting most of our anesthetics and medications due to the abnormalities of his blood type, molecular structure and just about everything else. It's like this person wasn't even around for the mandatory city shots every year that keep people from being this way."

Dr. Cross placed a finger to his lips in thought before saying, "Keep trying. If this patient dies, consider the blue tag that will go on his toe to also be your termination notice. Is that understood?"

"Yes, sir," Ritu said before signing off.

Standing, Dr. Cross walked to the enormous window in his office that overlooked the city of Flagstaff from the fiftieth floor of the building dedicated to his research. Then a thought struck him.

"The shots, of course," he muttered to himself, shaking his head that he hadn't thought of it sooner. "Ritu," he said as his nurse's face appeared on the window in front of him. "I want you to give him the winter and summer shots but hold off on the spring shots until I get down there," Dr. Cross said as he fingered out a combination of letters and numbers on the window, the amber colored digits spreading across the glass as he tapped away. "This dosage I'm sending is a weak mixture, but I don't want him going into cardiac arrest."

"Yes, sir," Ritu said. "Do you want me to file him?"

Dr. Cross hit a last button before swiping his hand and sending the combination sliding to the far side of the window, exposing the darkened city once again. The reason she was asking was because most of the time files weren't created for patients or test subjects that either were soon to die or had a large casualty rate.

"Make him a special file and send it to my office," he said, sitting at his desk again in his dimly lit area where he spent most of his time. "File it under J two-zero-one-two."

"J2012 will be on your desk shortly, sir," Ritu said. "Anything else?"

Ritu was not only Dr. Cross's best student in his rather large and rather selective university he'd built over the years, but she was also someone he considered a friend or at least a confidant. He considered telling her that what was left of the man they pulled out of the explosion and had on life-support was in fact from another time.

"Not at the moment," he said, picking the gauntlet up from his desk. "I have some more research to finish up here then I'll be down."

Ritu signed off and the doctor pushed play on the gauntlet and settled back in his chair to listen to the remainder of Jericho Johnson's tale.

Perhaps the storyteller would still be alive after he'd finished.

Chapter 28

Juno Beach, Normandy, March 12, 1096 A.D.

Wow. Of all the places we could've jumped to, the dawning of the First Crusade wasn't at the top of my fair-weather list. The weather was actually not bad on the shores of Normandy, but the scene before us could've been a tad less foreboding, as it were.

The beach was packed with the common folk of the Middle Ages, standing shoulder to shoulder while they all looked toward the makeshift stage set up in the center of the throng of men, women, and children who were all mesmerized by the sole occupant of the wooden planks. The stooped individual happened to be Peter the Hermit, one of the most influential speakers France had to offer when it came to making lords, barons, and dukes leave everything behind to join the Crusade.

The Hermit was really getting into his sermon on the morals of Christians and how it was our very God-given right to save the Holy Land from the heathens. While preaching he waved at the enormous wooden cross that he brought with him on his campaigns for troops.

Actually, if not for the inconvenient slaughtering of three-thousand pilgrims in Jerusalem, the preaching of Peter the Hermit and Pope Urban II's supposed vision from God that included, but was not limited to, lots of dead Turks and heathens, the first Crusade wouldn't have happened.

We ended up landing away from the spectacle and I immediately checked the gauntlet, told the girls the date and that we had almost seven hours to burn before I asked Chloe, "How was Klaus able to find us?"

Chloe sat on a nearby stump and shrugged. "I'm not sure, but I remember my father saying that men weren't meant to jump from time to time so the effects it leaves, although they aren't harmful to anyone, can be traced sometimes."

Sighing, I sat beside her on the large stump. "Well, isn't that just peachy?" then I remembered something. "Klaus knows everything about me. He said he got your father to talk."

"He won't kill him," Chloe said, sounding like she was trying to convince herself instead of me. "His research is worthless without him."

"How was he able to bring troops with him? I thought only my gauntlet could do that."

Chloe shrugged again, not looking at me. "Nothing makes sense anymore, Jericho."

Piper was watching the vehement sermon with curiosity. "What is he talking about?"

The Hermit was, in fact, speaking plain English, his voice thick with a French accent as he explained aggressively just why staying here was not only craven, but against the very will of God. Upon stating this, over half the mob, no doubt smitten by the Hermit's words, screamed out, "GOD WILLS IT!"

I had forgotten that Piper couldn't speak English. Back in Flagstaff, I had imprinted every language I could think of, so I would've been good if Peter the Hermit had been speaking slang Cantonese mixed with Arabic. "He's trying to convince all these people to either pick up a sword and go to Jerusalem or drop their coins into his coffers to support the valiant men already fighting in the name of God."

"Odin?"

"No, Piper, this God actually exists," I told her, scanning the crowd.

Chloe looked at me incredulously, like she couldn't believe I'd just said that to a pagan from birth. Noticing her stare of unbelief, I said, "We've already had this conversation on a long fishing trip. She's cool with it."

Nodding in agreement, Piper added, "Odin never died for anyone. Much less dying for the whole world."

"Don't get too zealous, Pipe. These people are already zealous enough. If they heard you speaking a different language they'd probably burn you at the stake."

After we'd sat and watched the rather long sermon, (these guys weren't your everyday one-hour-service kind of folks, it seemed), Chloe asked me, "Why did you come here in the first place?"

We were all lined up on the large stump with me in between them as I explained that I'd come because I was checking to see if William the Conqueror's son, Robert, was here. I also told them that the books had him in Normandy but were a tad vague as to when, where, and why.

"He was supposedly so poor when he departed for the Holy Land that it was said he had one change of clothes and no money at all. That'd be something to see, wouldn't it? A king with nothing to his name."

"A king with nothing is just a man," Piper decided to throw in, busting my bubble.

I glanced at her. "Try telling these people that," I said. "And I suppose he wasn't exactly the king even though by birthright he should've been. Speaking of which," I checked my gauntlet. We had plenty of time left. "Who wants to help me look for him?"

"Do you even know what he looks like?" Chloe asked while giving the rather large crowd a doubtful glance.

"Not exactly," I said, following her gaze to the large throng. "But I've met his dad once, so let's hope he doesn't look like his mother, Matilda."

Piper just shrugged at my idea while Chloe said, "Anything is better than just sitting here. As long as we aren't burned at the stake."

We went toward the cluster of tents and were able to enter the town without incident by heading around the people who seemed to still be having church and shouting "God wills it" at the top of their lungs.

I wasn't sure what we were supposed to do once we were inside but figured anything would beat the heck out of watching Peter the Hermit swindle men out of their lives and coins with his sermon. We entered through a stone gateway and found that the rather spacious little city was bustling with life even though it looked like every living soul within miles was listening to the loud preaching just outside.

We crossed the street to one side and began passing by all the local vendors who were selling everything from meat on a stick, linen, livestock, and even women. The progression of men and women selling their wares lasted a while, but we finally reached the end and turned on the next street.

Piper seemed to be having a good time, strangely, as she looked left and right, shaking her head at the vendors offering their furs and strange meats. My gaze lingered on her for some reason and she noticed, smiling brightly at me.

"These will look lovely in your beautiful hair, lass," an older flower-woman said to Piper, holding out a small white flower to her.

"She doesn't speak English," I told her. "But I agree. How much for the flower?"

"Nothing for her, sir," the old woman cackled. Her black hooded garb didn't look the cleanest, but she seemed nice enough.

Piper took the flower and nodded to the old woman as we passed by. Chloe wasn't exactly living in the moment so most of the vendors that tried to get her attention didn't even merit a glance.

I was about to tell her that being rude was just going to draw more attention to us, but our quiet span or luck ran out when we turned a corner in the street and saw Klaus and his goons standing in front of us.

Chapter 29

Before I had time to react, lots of bad things began happening at once. First of which was that all three Dragonovs began firing on us before I could shoot lightning at them, so retreat was the only option.

Turning quickly, I grabbed a female hand in each of mine and bolted down the street away from the Russians, sprays of bullets and a few rockets firing off after us.

Man, if we hadn't just turned a corner we would've been toast. It only helped momentarily, though, because we had been running past all of the vendors for less than three seconds before the Dragonovs were airborne, giving pursuit hard.

"Get down," Chloe screamed, dropping to the ground and snagging Piper and me by the ankles, resulting in us face-planting in front of her. Before I could tell her to chill out, I heard the unholy hiss of a rocket sizzle just above us, and a stall about twenty feet in front of us exploded, the man who had been selling fine fabrics spinning through the air.

Since we were all three lying down covering our heads like frightened children, we didn't get thrown across the town like the last time we'd encountered an exploding building. Getting to my feet, I hauled Piper up with me and we were running again.

"Do they even want the gauntlets intact?" I shouted above the roar of pandemonium that had ensued after Klaus had his men start sailing bottle-rockets from hell everywhere.

"Good question," Piper said from behind when we bolted into an alley. "We need horses."

"We can't outrun Dragonovs," Chloe told us fiercely. "The only chance we have is to obtain one of the suits ourselves."

The house we'd been leaning against while breathing like water buffalos shook and groaned. "I have to light them up again," I said quickly.

Chloe had already started shaking her head. "You can't. They're spread out this time and it takes them hours to reboot after a massive electrical jolt and we don't have time to wait for them. They've probably got their shields on now, anyway, after Scotland."

"Do they work like all good science-fiction and can withstand only so much?"

"No, they don't work that way. It's a self-sustaining type of shield that is the first of its kind."

"Let me guess. Your dad?"

Chloe nodded. "Afraid so."

"No sweet spot or anything?" I asked.

"Only that they're made to repel energy."

"Come again?"

"Things like bolts from the gauntlets or lasers."

"What about bullets?"

Chloe looked at me like I was asking one of the most foolish questions imaginable. "The Dragonovs don't have to repel bullets, Jericho," she said.

"What about a sword?" Piper asked.

Chloe sighed and was probably about to let her know that if bullets bounced off without leaving a scratch then swords sure weren't going to do any good in our endeavor, but I cut in.

"If Piper and I drew their attention, could you do anything from behind?"

We had long since started running again, and it wasn't making our planning any easier as we darted behind buildings and tents.

"Maybe," Chloe said, looking uneasy. "I've never had to work on one before, but my father said that if you take away all the bells and whistles, the Dragonov is just a more fire-power oriented version of the older STAf-7s. If that's the case, then—"

The building we'd been running close to shuddered and began collapsing. "Whatever, just do it," I shouted, shoving her on her way and bolting away with Piper close behind.

Splinters of wood and shards of rock hit us in the back

as the old structure groaned and fell right where we'd just been plotting. We skirted around the houses still standing and squatted behind a well. Peeking around the corner I saw that Klaus was still shouting at his devil soldiers and pointing at the rubble of the house they'd just brought down.

"What are you planning to do, Jericho?" Piper asked me just when we heard Klaus scream. "Just what is your plan, Johnson?"

"Geez, but will you people leave me alone and let me think?" I whispered furiously to Piper. "Stay here and don't come out till I say."

Before she could protest, I stood and walked out from behind the well with my hands up. "Let's chat, Klaus," I called, walking slowly toward him. All the Dragonovs started landing hard on the ground behind him, kicking up dust in their wake.

Turning, Klaus saw me and smiled. "You really have not grasped that your life means nothing to me, have you?" he said with his hands behind his back.

All three Dragonovs were covering him with their arms up and aimed right at me "Since your trigger-happy lunatics have killed both my comrades, I don't see why anyone else has to die," I said the lie rough and hard and Klaus took it.

"Both of them?" he asked.

"Yes," I said, hatred seeping from me. It wasn't exactly fake, either. This guy had probably just killed twenty to thirty people in less than thirty seconds.

"Even Atrium's girl?"

"Don't tell me you can't count to two."

"That's a shame," Klaus said, and he truly looked like he meant it as he frowned at the ground. "Chloe had a brilliant future ahead of her as the first of her kind. My only hope is that we can salvage her remains for another prototype." Then, to the two guards on his right he said, "Find her body."

Ever the picture of obedience, the two Dragonovs tromped off in search of Chloe's body because they needed it for…

What was he talking about, again?

I'm thinking I wasn't covering my facial features as good as I thought because Klaus noticed my darkened brow and said, "I take it she never explained to you that she's synthetic."

"Synthetic?" I asked, completely thrown off my groove, "Like an android?"

"However you wish to put it. Although, since she has functioning human parts riddled here and there throughout her metacore, she cannot be classified as an android or anything of the like."

Too fast. This was going way, way too fast.

Chloe came into my line of sight just then as she began sneaking up behind her target, the remaining Dragonov behind Klaus, and I couldn't help but notice how fluid her movements were.

Without thinking, my hand went to my right shoulder that still ached at times from when I had tackled her in Rome. I recall stating that she had to be wearing body armor. Not wanting to believe that I'd been tricked by some cheap rip-off, I grasped at anything I could think of. "But she bleeds. I saw that myself."

"From the neck up, yes," Klaus told me. "Minimum amount of blood and veins are required to keep the brain working properly and it also keeps all the mechanical fluids from the neck down at bay. Or somewhat, at least."

"Then how is she the first of her kind? Don't you future people have robots running out your ears?" I asked, watching in my peripheral vision as Chloe closed the gap between her and the unsuspecting pilot of the Dragonov.

"The real Chloe was killed in a raid when she was fifteen. Her body wasn't salvageable, but her father discovered her brain and a few other parts were. So after a year of testing, he created the being you've been running through time with for the past few days."

Fifteen. Told you I hated that number.

Chloe was almost there. "So her brain is all that's real?"

"That and her spine, which was the real breakthrough in

synthetics since hooking any kind of wires to a spine isn't easy and is also illegal," Klaus said.

It was true. All the insane feats I'd seen Chloe do came rushing back to me in one big picture.

"Now, I think this concludes our talk," Klaus said, extending his hand. "The glove, please."

Checking the glove, I saw we had three hours left. No hope of a last-minute train ride to safety this time. Chloe was standing right behind the Dragonov and seemed to be fiddling with the back plate without the soldier noticing.

Smiling, I asked, "Are you sure she's an android?" the Dragonov shook hard once with a jolt and collapsed to the ground as the eye pieces stopped glowing, "Because I think she's a flipping ninja."

Klaus spun around just in time to receive one of Chloe's classic perfect ten hurricane kicks to his chest. I couldn't help noticing that he flew almost fifteen feet before landing on the sandy street.

"Nice job, Robocop," I said, closing the gap between us and bending over to help her drag the pilot out of the Dragonov, which wasn't easy because he came out kicking and screaming, or he would've had not Chloe grabbed his neck when the chest piece opened up and, from what I could see from three feet away, crushed his windpipe.

"The other two are looking for what's left of your synthetic corpse. Won't take them long to realize you're still running on full battery," I told her, looking her up and down like I'd just met her.

Piper skidded to a stop beside us. "They're not far away. Whatever you're going to do, do it."

Chloe dragged the dead man out of the suit and motioned to me. "Get in," she commanded.

Not expecting this, I said, "Why me? You're the Terminatrix. You get in." It wasn't that I was trying to take jabs at her for not telling me or anything. I just truly and sincerely wanted her to pilot the Dragonov and save the day.

"I'm not synthetic, you idiot," she shouted. "The gauntlet needs to be protected so you've got to pilot this thing."

Without another word, I turned around and lay down in the suit, working my gauntleted hands into the arm slots. The armor closed around my legs, chest, and finally my face, and I took a deep breath.

"I don't know what I'm doing, here, Chloe," I said, my voice resounding through the helmet, sounding deeper and a tad amplified. It was dark inside the helmet until the eyes of the face mask turned on and the sky appeared. Lying there for a second, I saw a tiny loading sign spinning in the bottom right of my vision and a green bar came up beside a cloud, processed it, then the molecular structure of the cloud spilled out of the bottom of the green bar, explaining the various combinations required to create it.

I sat up. It felt like my real body when I placed a hand on the ground and got to one knee. The feeling isn't explainable, but I'll give it my best shot.

I felt like the mix of a Transformer, Spartan, and a ninja. Or, as I like to call it: Optimus Spinja.

I glanced at Chloe and more green bars appeared while the suit broke her down and informed me of her height, weight, and even put how much of a threat she was on a scale of one to ten.

She was around a two.

"You can tell it what to do in your mind if you are having doubts about commands," she said.

I had already figured this out when I had the suit make Chloe's skin disappear so I could get a look as her insides, which were all flesh and organs without any robotics to speak of.

On Chloe's end, I just looked like a tall-suited man staring at her through an expressionless helmet. But she knew what I was doing. Holding up her hands she said, "Satisfied?"

"Little bit," I said. "Did you say this thing can fly?"

Chloe nodded and started backing away, pulling Piper with her. "How does it work?" the Viking girl asked.

"Don't ask," Chloe told her. "Yes, it can fly," she tapped the side of her head. "Tell it in there and be careful."

Then she turned and both girls bolted away leaving me standing in the sandy street. Turning around, I started for Klaus, who was trying desperately to get to his feet. My steps made satisfying tromping sounds when I stopped next to him, reached down, and lifted him into the air by his coat collar.

I pulled his face close to my helmet and said, "Stay down, pal. Things are about to get ugly."

I guess I should have just dropped him but instead I reared him back and sent him skipping down the street like a rock on a pond.

"Stand down!" I heard the other Dragonovs yell from behind me. I turned my head to the side to look at them from over my shoulder.

"I said stand down!" one of them shouted again.

I faced them. "Anyone that don't figure on dying best slip out the back," I said in my most menacing Clint Eastwood voice before engaging the flight sequence in my mind.

I'm not sure what I was expecting. I mean, there were a lot of variables when it came to a manned suit flying such as jetpack, rocket boots, wings, jetpack with wings and such. I guess I was hoping for rocket boots to be honest. But when the red hologram wings sprouted from my back and the lower back of the suit blasted me into the air with twin ports shooting blue flames, I must say that the boots seemed a tad drab.

I whooped loudly while I climbed into the air at an almost sickening rate, if the feeling of all my organs slamming into my feet was anything to go by. After I'd ascended so high that the town looked like a speck of the shoreline, I leveled out and began to circle back to see if my enemies had followed me into the sky. I saw them coming fast and prepared myself for my first aerial combat.

The red holo-wings I'd thought were just for show were in fact the only way I could steer after I leveled out. Glancing at them in wonder, I saw that although I could see through them like any hologram, they were cutting the wind like butter. Then

I remembered what Chloe had said about the self-sustaining shield that could be engaged on the Dragonov and concluded that the wings could be something of the same material that had a limit to how far away it could go from my body.

Stopping in my soaring, I flapped my wings to stay in one place while the jetpack kept me hovering. Looking down past my feet dangling like church bells in the open air, I saw the other Dragonovs appear above the clouds not five-hundred yards right below me.

Each of them hissed off a missile at me and the right side of my viewing screen blinked red to let me know that both missiles were in fact locked onto me.

Awesome. Just when I was really starting to enjoy flying I had to try and shake off heat-seeking rockets with my name on them.

Peachy.

Chapter 30

Let me stop here for a few seconds to tell you, whoever-you-are, that all you're about to hear about my piloting skills is one-hundred percent true. If it sounds farfetched because you don't think I had the hours of practice like the other two schmucks had and that I even needed the hours of practice to survive, let me let you in on a little secret:

The Dragonovs weren't like flying a plane or playing a video game because I told it to do everything in my mind and it did it. If I didn't know a certain way of putting something so that the female computer voice would understand, I simply envisioned doing what I wanted in my head and it happened.

Sounds crazy, doesn't it? Well, it was crazy.

Crazy fun.

"Missiles inbound," the female computerized voice chirped.

"I know, I know," I growled, turning off the wings and flipping once before assuming a perfect dive toward the oncoming missiles. Just before they reached me, I turned on my right wing and flapped hard, spinning out of the way. My foes weren't expecting this and tried to fire off more shots, but I got to them first.

I don't know if you've noticed this, but I'm kind of a straightforward guy. So most of the time, without a plan in place as to what the heck I'm going to do, I just end up tackling stuff.

Literally.

I spread my arms wide before slamming into one of them hard, and the two of us spun through the air as we plummeted toward the sea. Punching, kicking, or any other methods of forceful attacks were useless against both of us, but that didn't stop us from trying. We beat at one another for a while and continued to drop to the black ocean, each trying to get in a good punch. Paying too much attention to beating my enemy's brains out and paying zero attention to the fact that we were running out of open air was just one of the reasons we landed in the cold waters of Normandy and began sinking fast like the hunks of metal we were.

Lights on the sides of our helmets automatically came on as we sank into the dark water. The female voice chirped every time we went down another ten feet, which was annoyingly a lot because we sank so fast. Then my opponent finally shoved me away and turned on his jetpack, floating in place while I kept sinking.

"Lock onto target," I said, holding up both arms.

I guess he figured out what I was doing because he blasted off, rocketing to the top of the sea. Blasting off after him, I kept my arms up and let my targeting system do its thing.

"Target locked," it beeped.

"Fire," I said, and two heat-seekers fired off from my wrists.

What? Just two?

"Keep firing, you crazy computer lady," I yelled as four more missiles hissed away after my target.

"Better?" it asked, shocking me.

"Uh," I muttered before my missiles hit the escaping suit, and what was left of the man began sinking in a flaming mass. Apparently the Dragonov shields weren't made to withstand the amount of firepower they carried themselves. "Yeah, loads. Thanks for asking."

I shot out of the water like a speeding bullet (you're going to say nothing of that comment) and started looking for the last bogey. Climbing higher into the sky, I found he wasn't in sight. Then I remembered that I was flying in state-of-the-art battle armor.

"Find him," I said, stopping in the air to hover. When nothing happened I said, "Uh, locate nearest enemy?"

Still nothing.

I thought for a second before trying a few other

commands, with no results. If my computer voice hadn't beeped informing me of incoming missiles, I might never have found him. Red dots zipped toward me on my targeting screen.

Blasting off I said, "Deploy counter measures."

It was a perfectly logical command I thought because it stood to reason that anything that flew and shot weapons had to have counter measures, right?

Wrong.

Apparently the Dragonov didn't rock counter measures or anything resembling them.

Barrel-rolling to my left, I gritted my teeth and spun, just waiting for one of the small missiles to hit me. None of them did, shockingly, and they hissed past me. I stopped spinning and turned to see the last enemy flying toward me.

"Any other weapons besides missiles?" I asked.

"Please select from the following options." The female voice told me and a list of what I was assuming were weapons appeared on the screen that also included the rushing Dragonov almost upon me.

Scanning the list in panic, I randomly picked one, shouting, "Saber rounds!"

"Saber rounds selected. Auto-locking target."

I was not disappointed.

Two thick, eight-barreled mini guns appeared from somewhere on the back of my suit and lowered down over my shoulders. The opposing Dragonov didn't stand a chance once the computer had locked onto him and I'd started firing. Unlike normal Gatling style weapons that fire at a severely rapid rate, these little jewels, which were shooting armor piercing rounds, fired at an almost slow pace considering the type of weapon that they were.

Something beeped loudly and the voice in my head said, "Target has deployed self-destruct. Would you like a suggestion?"

The almost sing-song way the computer spoke was a little disconcerting, but since I did have a falling apart hunk of almost exploding metal almost upon me, I shouted, "Yes," covering the eyes of my helmet against the coming kamikaze.

The suggestion, as the voice put it, was in fact the shutting off of my boosters and holo-wings, causing me to instantly drop, and the other flaming Dragonov passed just overhead whilst I pin wheeled down. I was probably thirty feet underneath it when the self-destruct happened, the force of the explosion sending me speeding downward in crazy cartwheels before I landed back in the ocean.

Our aerial fight had brought us close to the shoreline it seemed because I hit bottom hard, landing on my back while sand kicked up all around me. I lay there for a second trying to take in all that had just happened in the last five minutes before groaning and getting to my feet. Looking up, I saw that I was in about fifteen feet of water. Deciding that I'd had enough flying for the time being, I began walking slowly toward the bank, my feet tearing through the weak seaweed and scaring fish away from their homes.

It was kind of peaceful, actually, trudging under the water in semi slow-motion after I'd just handed two deadly soldiers their own butts. Little pieces of shrapnel began dropping into the water above me, swirling past me, or landing on my helmet and shoulders with a soft clink before settling on the bottom.

It was strange to think that hundreds of years from now some intrepid explorer might find the remains of 23rd century battle armor under the waves and think it to be something else entirely.

My helmet was out of the water by that time, and I saw Chloe and Piper standing on the beach. Hoping I looked half as boss as I felt whilst marching out the sea, I approached them, stopping ankle deep in foam in front of the spectators.

"Are you alright?" Chloe asked with a look of sincere worry. "It looked like it got a little rough up there."

I shrugged, causing the whir of gears with the motion. "Nothing I couldn't handle," I said, suddenly serious when a notion struck me. "Chloe, these things can't fall into the wrong hands. I knew it wasn't a great idea in the first place, but after using one I really know we can't let Klaus win."

"I know," Chloe said, nodding. "Klaus is gone. He jumped a few seconds after we took the Dragonov."

"Where could he have gone?" Piper asked. "Don't you have what he wants?"

"Power down," I said as the suit sank to its knees, the chest and arms opening, allowing me to step out on the sand.

Then I fell down.

Chloe and Piper both grabbed under my arms and lifted me to my feet. "Careful, Jericho," Chloe told me. "You're going to have to walk slowly for a minute."

All feelings of my heroism were gone after having to loop each of my arms around a girl's neck to walk. They seemed to be the only viewers to bear witness to my feats of aerial combat because the sermon being held by Peter the Hermit was still in full swing with the crowd still shouting, "God wills it.

It was for the best, I suppose. Had any want-to-be pilgrims saw the three-winged demons flying overhead whilst the Hermit spoke, they might've changed their tunes from amen to burn him.

We finally made it back to the stump we'd been sitting on before all Helheim broke loose, and I gratefully sat back down slowly. I wasn't sore or anything, just wobbly. I was, however, able to walk the last ten of fifteen feet to the stump without the aid of my female crutches, so I guess that was a plus.

The three of us sat in silence for a few minutes, choosing to stare at the ocean this time instead of the multitude of people. When my gauntlet said two hours left, I broke the silence. "So, why'd Klaus think you were synthetic?" I asked, keeping my eyes on the sea.

Chloe didn't answer right away and I'm thinking she was probably trying to think of the best way of telling an uncomfortable story. "He was talking about Beck, my sister."

"Beck," I repeated, looking at her. "Like, little sister, twin sister?"

"Identical twin," she confirmed.

Piper hadn't heard Klaus's speech, so she just sat there watching us talk about things she didn't understand. Poor thing.

Since I didn't want to leave her completely out, I leaned slightly in her direction and touched my shoulder to hers. "Was everything he said about the raid when she was fifteen true, then?"

"In a roundabout way, yes," she said, leaning forward and putting her elbows on her knees. "The explosion that killed her happened when she was twenty, but she'd been missing since she was fifteen."

"Why?"

Chloe shrugged. "Beck was always the more rebellious of the two of us, but the real reason was she met someone handsome who turned out to be a Rebel and she ran away with him."

"Tough break. But that still doesn't explain why Klaus thought you were her."

"Father was always a recluse, and since we were his daughters, so were we. When you live in a war-ridden city where you don't go out unless you're killing something, it's not hard to hide the fact that you have more than one child, which is illegal," Chloe said.

Wow. Way to cut down on population growth. "But if there's a law saying you can only have one child isn't there like a fallback plan for people who have twins?"

"Apparently not," Chloe said. "Our father was a renowned scientist, so he was a public figure. And since he didn't want to keep us locked up like animals he alternated taking one of us with him," she smiled then at some memory before saying, "After years of this it became almost like a currency between us. We would trade each other turns or give them to each other in exchange for something. Beck was quite the business woman because she went more than me in our teens," her smile faltered. "Then one day she went and never came back."

"Just like that?" I asked, frowning, "She never told you any plans of, I don't know, ditching you guys for Romeo the Rebel?"

"No."

"When was she wounded?" Piper asked, sounding cute considering the wound she was referring to was in fact death, dismemberment, and reanimation but hey, she was a Viking, cut her a break.

"Five years later. Beck was the commander of the raiding party attacking our supply lines, and I was sent to stop her. I didn't know it was her until I got close and she lifted her helmet to ask how father was doing," Chloe face darkened, and I was beginning to think that maybe I shouldn't have opened this particular can of worms but, since I was nosy, I asked, "What happened then?"

"Then her team and my team fought, my team won, and I carried her remains back to my father," Chloe said this in a very hard sort of way, like she was starting to feel annoyed at the subject but didn't want to stop. "Father couldn't have saved her without the help of his estranged colleague Dr. Cross. So after a few days in the lab, Beck was fully functional, with the exception of having her memories of the Rebels wiped. Since Dr. Cross, father, and I were the only ones who even knew that she'd vanished five years prior, there wasn't any danger of her identity getting out if we started switching places again. The problem came when my father realized that I was now a field scientist with my own platoon and couldn't just switch places with my newly synthetic sister anymore. So after Beck had paced the floors on lockdown for a few weeks she disappeared again. It was during those weeks when Klaus showed up unexpectedly and caught my father tweaking a few wires on Beck's arms. That's why he thinks I'm synthetic."

It was a rather long story for such a short question, but I was about as enlightened as I was going to get, it seemed. I wanted to ask what she and her father felt throughout the course of it, though, because she told the facts straightforward and left out all emotions attached.

Like, did she and her sister have a good relationship? Did she think daddy loved Beck more? Was she glad her sister was gone? I wanted to ask all of those questions until I saw a tear slip down Chloe's cheek and all of them were answered.

I didn't know what to say so I said, "You don't know where she went?"

Chloe sniffed and shrugged again. "Erasing selected memories isn't easy and there's always a chance that they'll come back. My guess is that they did and she went back to the Rebels."

"And since Klaus didn't know about her, he thinks you're synthetic," I said.

Chloe nodded. "It's one of the reasons he sent me after you. To see what I could do."

I stood and walked a few steps away. "Where do you think he went?"

"I don't know," Chloe said.

"He really has to be stopped."

"You think I don't know that?"

"Then think, Chloe. Where would he go if he was running for his life?" I asked.

Chloe looked toward the town that Klaus had fled from, "There are so many places he could've gone. But he most likely would've gone to a place where he could get more men."

"Flagstaff?" I asked, checking my right gauntlet. "Not like we could follow him if we wanted to."

"This might be our last random jump, though," Chloe reminded me. "Father said two or three. It's been three so maybe we're going back to Flagstaff anyway."

"You mean Flagstaff two years later. The place where I die, remember?" I said. "Your dad also said that I hated Klaus more than anything and I got to say, if we jump in the next few minutes straight to Flagstaff, I don't think I meet the criteria on that yet. I mean, don't get me wrong, I think he's a complete jerk, for an evil world-dominating mastermind, but your dad's description of me isn't the way I feel right at the moment."

Maybe it was because Chloe didn't think I was head-over-heels in love with her or Piper that made her look at me the way she did then, but after I saw her face, the only logical place I could think of that Klaus would go suddenly came into my mind.

"No," I muttered, my skin chilling as I stood. "We have to follow him."

"Jericho, we don't know if we can," Chloe said, standing and holding her arms out to me the way a negotiator might to a suicide bomber.

"Your dad said something about jumps leaving traces. Where'd he jump from?" I was almost shouting now.

"Somewhere in the street but we don't know that he—"

I bolted for the town with Chloe and Piper calling after me to stop and was out of breath by the time I reached the sandy street that I'd thrown Klaus in. A few buildings and houses were still smoldering in piles after the Dragonov raid and all the people that were still alive had vanished somewhere to hide.

Not knowing what I was looking for or how to look for it, I began walking around in a long circle, holding up my right glove like it was a cell phone and I needed bars. Then, miraculously because of how foolish I felt, I did indeed get bars. The gauntlets screen that had been counting down the time left in 1096 vanished and was replaced by a sentence stating that I was in range of a jump site.

Bingo.

A red marker appeared that worked like a compass and after a minute of walking around I stopped when it glowed green and said a jump had happened there almost forty minutes ago. I glanced around. It didn't look any different at first but then I saw the air shimmer like a heat wave a few feet away.

Then the date of the jump appeared, confirming my fears.

Chicago, Illinois, August 4, 2012.

Then another blip appeared on the screen that asked if I would like to travel to this destination.

Before I could select yes or no, a Dragonov landed beside me, causing a crater in the middle of the street and scaring me to death. The helmet opened and I saw Chloe's face. "Is it giving you an option to follow him?

I nodded.

Piper appeared beside me, grabbing my arm. "Then let's go."

Chloe laid an armored hand on my other shoulder and I selected yes on my glove.

Apparently it was time to go.

Chapter 31

I ran away from my foster home once when I was ten years old. The pressure of being that young and also being in the tenth grade was a tad much, I guess, because I packed my backpack with four PBJs and two liters of Kool-Aid and struck out alone in the small town of Pelahatchie, Mississippi. I left a note for my foster mother, where I thought she'd see it on the counter a few feet away from where she was gabbing away on a cord phone and left.

My adventure, which consisted of being told, "Go home, kid. You bother me," by the busman and being chased by two Doberman Pinschers a few neighborhoods over, was a short one, indeed, but I would have soldiered on had not one key factor happened that made me rethink my escape of reality.

I ran out of Kool-Aid.

That, whoever-you-are, was my cue to call it a day and go home.

Oh, yeah. I guess I never told you that whoever my parents were, they left me at an orphanage when I was a newborn. I was a real-life baby-on-the-doorstep, they told me.

The only real setback this caused in my life of perfection was that I couldn't go to college at twelve when I graduated and had to wait until I was fifteen. Other than that, I've been great. I guess if I hadn't spent so much time with my face in books, and I mean a lot of books, I might've wondered more about why I was dumped and who had done the monstrous deed.

Repressed? Maybe. I like reformed better.

When I arrived back home about an hour later, drenched in sweat from running from the hellhounds, I went in to explain to Maryann, my foster mom, that I didn't mean what I'd written in the note and that I'd also like some more grape Kool-Aid.

Except she was still laughing away on the phone and

hadn't even seen the note.

Having to come home because I was out of delicious grape-flavored water (unlikely because I now hate Kool-Aid and have banned it from my mansion) would've been great this time around instead of coming home to try and save the lives of the only two people in 2012 that I actually cared about.

We were ready for anything when the three of us phased into Chicago. I glanced around and saw that we happened to be standing right behind my favorite coffee shop on this side of town. Mikey's Place.

It was great that we didn't land in the middle of a highway and get hit like three drunk time-traveling bums by oncoming traffic and all, but it was horrifying that Klaus had landed only a street over from my house.

I looked us over to see how we'd make out in a coffee shop and noticed that we didn't look bad for people from three different times.

No. We looked way worse than that.

Piper was bad enough because she was wearing leather armor and the pelts of wolves—yes, flipping *wolves*—but Chloe was worse because, unless you forgot what you just heard not five minutes ago, she was wearing an eight-foot tall suit of black power-armor.

Then the suit disappeared right before my eyes. What the heck?

"How's that?" I heard Chloe's voice say.

"Of course it can turn invisible," I muttered. "Your old man really made these little jewels a regular Swiss Army knife, didn't he?"

"Something like that. The cloak only lasts ten minutes, though."

Piper, who had by this time seen too much science-fiction and was therefore unimpressed, said, "This is where you're from, Jericho?"

Nodding, I glanced around. "Yep. The economy blows, the government is a tad tyrannical at times, and healthcare is a nightmare, but it's home, I guess," then I turned to where I thought Chloe was. "Take the gauntlets and get into the sky. Piper and I are going through this shop, and my house is just on the other side of the street so meet us at my steps."

"Her clothes…" Chloe's voice said. "I lived in 2012 long enough to know she might get a bucket of red paint on her."

"I'm rich," I said, glancing at Piper's getup again. "I'll say we're flying to a Renaissance festival tonight or something."

"Be careful," Chloe said, taking the gloves I held out to her. They vanished into what I was guessing was a compartment on the Dragonov before I heard the quiet hum of her taking off. Funny how the sounds of a busy city can hide the sounds of a jetpack.

I grabbed Piper's hand. "You're with me, sweetheart. Try and act natural and leave the talking to me."

Piper nodded but was looking at our hands clasped together. Opening the back door, I stepped in and pulled her in behind me. The aroma of caffeinated goodness flooded my nostrils and I almost died from the heavenly scent. Man, I could've used a good cup of coffee.

We entered the shop area and I was recognized instantly by a lot of the patrons. I had forgotten that I left with Chloe almost two months ago and to these people I'd been MIA for that long.

Of course, I guess it was kind of true.

We walked past the counter as the cameras began flashing. "Evening, Charlie," I said to the smiling girl.

"How are you this evening, Mr. Johnson?" she asked.

Before I could tell her that I'd been better she blurted, "And where have you been for the past two months?"

Since I hadn't been expecting to lie so quickly, I went with the first thing I could think of. "Visiting my hot Norwegian model girlfriend," I said, putting an arm around Piper's fur-clad shoulders. "We're off to a Ren-fest as you can see."

Reporters frequented Mikey's Place because of me, and since I'd been gone for a few months, the place was crawling with them just hoping for a glance of me, I guess.

Well, a glance they did get and then some as they blocked the door when I tried to exit with my arm linked through Piper's.

"How long have you been modeling?" one asked, holding a recorder toward her.

"Just say anything politely," I said to her in Scandinavian. "They won't know the difference."

"You all smell terrible," Piper told them, her native language sounding ever so wonderful to the greedy reporters even though they couldn't understand a single word of it.

"She says since last January," I said.

"How long have you been together?"

"Feels like hundreds of years," I answered, pushing through the throng.

"Is she the one, Jericho?" a woman asked with her recorder out.

"Maybe. I do know that I'd travel through time and space just to be with her," I said, smiling back at her, and even though she didn't understand a word I was saying, she smiled back.

A chorus of "aws" and "oohs" went up throughout the crowd of reporters. Pressing my way through them I said, "That's all. You guys wait here and I'll be right back."

Cameras were still flashing when the two of us exited the buzzing coffee shop and walked across the semi-busy street, stopping at my steps. All looked quiet inside.

I guess this is a good time to interject where most of my funds came from. I want you to think of the stock market, horse racing, the super-bowl, the lottery and just about every other gambling event you can think of. Got it? Now, I want you to think of the only person you know of that has ways of finding out what the stocks, horse races, super-bowl and lottery are going to do tomorrow. Got that one?

I think that's enough explaining, actually. If you haven't figured it out by now, then I don't think there's any hope for you.

But a lot of it came from stocks.

"What's the plan?" I heard Chloe's voice ask from the

middle of the steps somewhere ahead of us.

I tried to walk past her but ended up bumping into her stupid invisible armor and almost falling backwards. "Watch where I'm going, for God's sake," I told her, finishing the climb to my door with Piper behind me.

The door was ajar and had bullet holes in it.

We entered slowly with me glancing left and right for any signs of a crazy Russian guy with a gun.

Chloe was still cloaked when she came in behind us and closed the door. It took us almost fifteen minutes to sweep the whole house before we could deduce that Klaus wasn't there.

And neither was Evonne or Louise.

The girls didn't think that was a big deal. So I told them that they both lived there and, since they were old, never exactly left at night to go on the prowl and paint Chicago red.

"How would you know?" Chloe asked, visible now because she'd shut off the cloak to let it recharge, climbing out of it when it powered down in my boasting room. "You don't look the type to give them the night off much."

After I decided that the Dragonov looked like it should be a permanent piece in my enormous living room, I said, "I'm an awesome boss, Chloe. But I've technically been gone for two months so all bets are off."

"What about your lab?" Chloe asked.

"We can look but Klaus couldn't have gotten in without me being here—" I froze.

I was walking toward the door that lead to the elevator to my lab when I noticed the sheet of paper taped to it.

"Master Johnson," it started. "'Verde' von Klaus is having me write this down to inform you that he is taking myself and Miss Louise to your college classroom. He says to bring him the gauntlets or he shall kill both of us."

And, just in case I didn't take the note seriously enough, there was blood smeared on the bottom half of it and another sentence was written in Russian.

This blood belongs to the old woman. Hurry.

I crumpled the letter and held it against my head in a balled fist before roaring and punching the door it had been taped to, bruising my knuckles. "He has them," I said hoarsely.

"What do we do?" Chloe asked, all business.

Right then, at that moment, I hated Klaus more than anything. Which meant that my demise may or may not have been creeping closer. But to Helheim with that. It was flipping go time.

"Chloe, take Piper to one of the rooms and find her something current to wear while I go to the lab for a second. I got weapons to grab."

Once I was in the lab I set to work selecting weapons from my old and new collections. After I'd grabbed two handguns and ammo clips, I started rummaging through the medieval pile, selecting a longsword for Piper and even a belt of throwing knives since I knew she was deadly with them. Chloe wasn't going to need weapons since she was in the Dragonov, but I'd grabbed an assault rifle just in case.

Then I headed for the elevator again.

"I'm coming, guys," I said to the ether, willing Evonne and Louise to hear me. "Hang in there."

Chapter 32

Piper and I took a cab while Chloe followed us in a cloaked Dragonov from above. After I dropped two-thousand dollars in the cabbie's lap and told him to drive like a maniac, I closed the passenger shield and put in earbuds. We were screeching away headed to the college.

Piper kept the questions about everything we passed to the minimum to, I don't know, not bother me, I guess. Which was kind of relieving but also not because I didn't want her to think she couldn't talk to me when she wanted.

"What's on your mind, Piper?" I asked.

She'd changed into a pair of faded jeans and a lime green American Eagle t-shirt. I noticed she was also wearing a pair of blue Converse that Chloe had dug up from somewhere, which seemed to go too well with the rest of her ensemble and made me wonder who had picked the outfit. "I was thinking how comfortable these shoes are," she said, peering down at her feet past the broadsword that was riding between her knees.

Wow. The way she was dressed and wielding a sword was something out of my wildest, nerdiest dreams.

"They're great, right?" I said. "I wore these things long before I bought half the company that makes them. They can't be beat, really."

Then I realized that I had probably sounded conceited by the mentioning of buying half of Converse. "You are very rich, aren't you, Jericho?" Piper asked, looking up from her feet to me.

Great. I knew I'd sounded conceited.

"I get by."

"How?" she asked.

Opening the small duffel bag, I pulled out the glove that had started it all. "Because of this," I said, handing it to her. "I use it to go forward a day or so sometimes to predict the future.

Knowledge like that in my time is quite lucrative."

"And the people of your time don't know about this?"

"Nope," I said, glancing out my window. We were almost to the college.

"So you're a fraud," Piper said, and I noticed it wasn't a question but her just laying out all the facts and giving it a name.

I bobbed my head in indecisive fashion before saying, "I wouldn't say fraud, per se. Maybe just well informed."

"But you lie when people ask how you do it, right?"

I was starting to not like this conversation very much. "Well, yeah, but only because other people don't need to go back in time at will, Piper."

"And you can?" she asked, passing the gauntlet back to me.

I wasn't ready for this talk with anyone yet. The only two people that knew about me before had been Evonne and Louise, and since they were basically millionaires themselves because they worked for me, neither of them had tried to give me the moral decision talk.

And here I was, in the back of a cab with a beautiful Viking girl and she was making me feel like the biggest liar to date.

And yes, whoever-you-are, I do in fact know that I kind of am the biggest liar to date.

"Listen, Piper, I know this may sound lame, but there was a reason I found the gauntlet and no one else did. It was half-buried in the bushes on a nature trail frequented by thousands of regulars every day. Why was I, the man who hates nature trails and was only there to meet a buddy from college, the one to find it? I'm not one to talk about the fates or whatever, but if Chloe's dad hadn't hid the glove from Klaus, the world as we know it would've been toast a long time ago."

Before I knew it, I had grabbed her hand. "You told me once that none of this was my responsibility and that may be. But if I, the one who found the glove and kept Klaus from screwing up the planet in the first place, don't try and stop him, who will? And since your time won't be ruined by Klaus, it's you who have the best reasons to not be helping me do this."

Our eyes were locked when I finished, and we didn't hear the cab driver tell us that we were at our stop while we took in each other's face.

"I really like you, you know," she said, her mouth curving slightly in a smile when she repeated the words that had haunted me since she'd last spoke them on our frigid fishing trip. "That's why I'm here, Jericho. Whatever you decide after this is all over, I'm just glad that the great Jericho Johnson took the time to stop by my small village."

Then she leaned toward me slowly, our eyes still locked, and I leaned toward her slowly, our heads turned perfectly for the long-awaited, time-defying kiss.

But right before one of the best moments of my life was complete, someone knocked on my passenger door.

I'm not one to stop mid magical first kiss and certainly not one to stop post magical first kiss. But since we did have an evil lunatic trying to kill us on the loose, I did stop, turning to see who the buzz-kill of an intruder was.

"If the two of you are quite done it seems we've arrived," Chloe said curtly from the other side of the window.

Geez. I would've preferred Klaus instead of Chloe right about then. God knows it wouldn't have been near as embarrassing.

I nodded and Chloe turned in her invisible Dragonov and headed up the steps to the college. I went to open the car door, but Piper still had one of my hands. Pulling it to her lips, she planted a kiss on my hand. "We'll talk."

The door was kicked in and we entered the college.

Darkened halls were what greeted us and since I wasn't in ninja mode I turned on a light every time we passed a switch toward my classroom.

"How do you want to play this, Jericho?" Chloe asked.

"What do you mean?" I muttered, checking other rooms as we passed for Klaus just in case.

"We can't give him the glove," she said simply.

I stopped walking and turned to the girl beside me in the

enormous battle suit. "We also can't let him kill my friends, Chloe."

"Fair enough," Chloe said, vanishing before me. "I'll move in when I can."

The journey to my room seemed to take longer than I remembered it taking when Piper and I stopped at my door. Taking a deep breath, I pushed into the room, with my gun ready.

"Jericho," Klaus said to me, like he was addressing a long-lost colleague. "Nice of you to join us."

Evonne and Louise were on their knees in front of the madman, a pistol at the back of each of their heads. "Let them go," I said automatically, with Piper beside me ready to spring into action, her broadsword held up.

"You had three minutes until you would have found their corpses. Cutting it a little close, are you not?" then he scanned the room and added, "Where is Chloe?"

"She's back at my house in case you showed your ugly mug back there first," I told him, edging to my right, my pistol still pointed toward him.

Although this sounded like the truth because I had thought about leaving one of the girls behind for that reason, Klaus wasn't buying it. "You care for too many people in this room, Jericho. Here," he said, cocking one of his guns. "Allow me to help you think faster."

Then he shot Louise.

The older woman cried out, landing on the hard floor. He hadn't mortally wounded her, but since she wasn't the youngest of women, he probably didn't have to.

Evonne went to help her, but Klaus cocked the gun and held it against his head. "Don't even think it," he told him, and Evonne resumed his kneeling with his hands on his knees. "Everyone else but you out of the room, now," he told me.

"I'm going to kill you," I said low and dangerous, stepping closer to the horrifying scene. "She's an old woman, for God's sake."

Klaus leveled a gun at me this time. "I'm tired of your

games. Now you can finally see that I am done playing them. The glove. Now," he said, motioning the gun toward a desk a few feet in front of him.

"Chloe," I said aloud, starting for the evil man, "Come out, please, and don't try anything. I don't want anyone else hurt."

It took a few seconds for Chloe to realize that I was serious, and she appeared to my right halfway between Klaus and me.

"Leave," I told the girls. Piper wasn't thrilled about it, but she exited with Chloe tromping behind her.

"A wise decision," Klaus stated once the door closed behind them. "See? All you needed was a push in the right direction," then he kicked at Louise's feet.

"Leave her alone," I said.

"The glove."

"Let Mitch go first," I tried.

"No."

"Mitch first," I shouted.

Klaus smiled at me. "Sometimes people don't get what they want, boy."

"You're right," I said, producing the gauntlet from my duffel bag, placing it on the desk and aiming my gun at it.

"It won't matter. Sparks will just make another once you're dead," Klaus said although he wasn't smiling anymore.

"Is that so?" I said, sounding more in control of my voice now. "Then why didn't he after this little jewel vanished?"

His face darkened and I kept going. "Oh, that's right, because there isn't any more Z-90 to make one."

Klaus growled low and I saw a muscle jerk in his jaw. Then he grabbed Evonne's shoulder. "On your feet."

"I'm so glad you're not wearing those heinous wind pants you wore when you visited Nero, Master Johnson," Evonne said, getting to his feet slowly, his eyes on me. "Terribly inconvenient in a tussle, wouldn't you say?"

Klaus's eyes were on the glove beside me, and he either didn't hear what Evonne had just told me to do or just didn't care that we were talking.

But I knew what he was trying to tell me.

And all Helheim was about to break loose.

Klaus shoved him on his way, and after he'd taken a few steps away and blocked me from the madman's line of sight, I sprang into action.

When Evonne and I had been captured and brought before Nero, the crazed emperor thought we were spies and had everyone else leave the room so he could personally question us due to the fact that he didn't trust anyone in his court.

To make a long story short, Nero had produced a sword and tried to make us talk that way. Since we were weaponless and I was completely out of ideas, I did the only thing that I could think of to gain the upper-hand.

I shoved Evonne into Nero.

Hard.

It wasn't among the pantheon of all my normally glorious short-notice plans and it did in fact end with us escaping, but it was a half-cocked, crazy plan that Evonne had made me promise never to do again.

Ha.

I shoved Evonne as hard as I've ever shoved another human being in my life and the effects were absolutely magical, if I do say so myself. Both men ended up barreling over backwards and over the top of the line of desks behind them.

Klaus's gun went off when they landed, and a light fixture exploded to my left. Roaring, Klaus went to throw Evonne off him but suddenly got a taste of what happens when my butler gets severely put off by someone. Evonne sat up before swiveling and planted the most sickening sounding elbow to the man's face before rolling off him and prying the gun out of his hands, standing and holding the weapon on Klaus.

I guess he thought I was done and that's why he decided to hold him at gunpoint, so I could take a minute to think and devise the best way to end this drama.

"Get Louise out of here," I said, slipping my glove back on and mounting the dazed Russian's chest. I grabbed his collar, pulled him to me, and smashed my now metal-clad fist into his face as hard as I could.

Somewhere in the middle of me beating Klaus to a pulp, Evonne carried Louise out of the room. On my seventh or eighth punch Klaus caught my glove in his, jerking me sideways and somehow slamming me on the side of my face on the floor, sticking me with the most painful of jabs in my side.

I roared, swiveling one of my legs, and wrapping it around Klaus's head, flipping him over and putting the squeeze on him.

And also, the next time you're trying to kill someone by choking them to death with your legs around their neck, make sure that the man/woman silently trying to pry your legs away is *not* wearing a scandium gauntlet with razor sharp fingertips.

Just saying.

I gritted my teeth against the agony and possibly might have seen stars when Klaus turned all five points to my right leg, biting them deep into my thigh.

My vision blurred when Klaus squeezed the points deeper into my thigh and all I could see was my blood going everywhere. There comes a moment in every fight when one of the fighters passes the point of not caring and I have to say that when I turned my body hard just so that my gushing blood would pour all over Klaus's battered face, I was well past it.

Speaking of blood, I'd lost a lot of it from my mangled and shredded leg judging by my starting to black out. The last thing I remembered was rolling my wobbling head down to see Klaus's bloodied face vanish and Chloe busting through the door and screaming something I didn't understand.

Maybe it was something akin to, "Heavens, Jericho is lying in a pool of his own blood and Klaus just got away again!"

At least that's what I was hoping she was exclaiming in tears as she knelt beside me, shaking me hard by the shoulder with her massive Dragonov hand.

Because that's what felt like just happened.

And maybe a herd of rhinos had trampled me somewhere along the way, too.

Chapter 33

I awoke on a table. Not the best way to awaken, let me tell you. More so when you instantly try and sit up fast because you think you're still in mortal combat with a crazy Russian maniac in a college classroom.

"Easy, Jericho," Chloe said, placing her hands firmly on my bare chest to keep me from sitting up. "Be still, please. You're not ready to move yet."

The room we were in would've been pitch black if not for the only lamp across the room on the wall. I noticed that it flickered at times, as if the wiring wasn't the best or that it was old.

Then I noticed Chloe's hands still on my chest.

"Where are we?" I groaned, allowing her to push me back down on the table, which I realized was actually a hospital gurney. Chloe was sitting beside the uncomfortable bed.

"Flagstaff," she said, removing her cool hands from me and placing her arms on the side of the gurney, the black sleeves of her jumpsuit barely grazing my right arm.

"Okay, when are we?" I asked, closing my eyes because leaving them open was giving me a headache.

"2342."

I kept my eyes closed. "The year I die?"

"Jericho, this is where Klaus went. We had to follow him," Chloe said. "I don't know what's going to happen to us but I'm just glad that you're... you didn't..."

She was trying to look around the dimly lit room and not at me, which I was guessing was her way of not crying, a method that wasn't working at all because a tear escaped and landed on my shoulder.

"Cold hands and warm tears."

Chloe glared at me, more tears streaming. "Will you please

just try and be serious? I thought you were dead."

I sat up slowly, my face level with her glaring one due to the tall gurney. "I don't know, Chloe. Since I might be dead sometime soon I'd rather not be too serious. Might miss something," I said, trying to swing my legs off the gurney, except my right leg was strapped to the confounded thing.

"Say, Chloe?" I asked, frowning at... what the heck was that thing? "What's, uh, messing with my leg?"

It looked like a robot hand that was hooked to something that extended from the darkened ceiling. "It's fixing your leg. When it's done you'll be as good as new." Chloe said, glancing up at the arms base. "Except this is a rather old model and that's why it's taking twice as long. It's the only one the Rebels had."

"We're Rebels, now?" I said, flopping back onto the ragged gurney. "How'd that come about?"

Chloe sat back down and explained what had happened after I'd passed out in my classroom. Evonne had left for a hospital once he'd exited the room, loping down the hallway while carrying Louise.

"Was she alright?" I asked.

Chloe shrugged one shoulder slowly and shook her head. "We didn't stay around long enough to follow up. The gunfire had attracted the authorities and all we could do was use the gauntlet and follow Klaus."

Piper.

"Where's Piper?"

Chloe's face was impossible to read as she said, "Sleeping," she went on to explain we'd landed in the heart of Flagstaff after the jump and Klaus was waiting with a few guns. "We ran for a while before going into an access tunnel to the underground. I ended up having to self-destruct the Dragonov and seal us in to get away from them."

"So when did we turn Rebel?"

"They found us after an hour of wandering the tunnels. Things have changed in the past two years, Jericho. The Rebels aren't just flies to the Bears anymore. They're actually in the war," Chloe seemed bothered by this so I decided a change of subject was in order.

"I'm guessing you were the one carrying me the whole time the two of you were running for your lives," I said, taking her hand. "Listen, Chloe, I know our relationship hasn't been the best ride so far but, for what it's worth, I'm glad you didn't leave me to die in my own classroom."

Chloe looked incredulous. "How could I have left you?" she asked in a sort of quavering voice, placing a hand on the side of my face.

What was she doing?

"I don't know," I said, flicking my eyes left and right in a semi-uncomfortable fashion. "I suppose if the sight of blood was your Achilles—"

Then she smothered my lips with hers.

In case you love every word that I say and would hate to miss out on hearing me say one, I was, in fact, about to say the word heel.

The kiss was, well, to put it way mildly, unexpected. I felt like an idiot because my eyes were open and I could see that hers weren't. The kiss wasn't exactly a fun one nor was it a spontaneous, passionate one.

It was almost a harsh, hungry, needy type of kiss.

"I'm glad you're feeling better," a female voice said and the kiss ended abruptly. Chloe pulled her head back but didn't step away quickly like she'd been caught.

It was Piper standing at the entry way to the medical room, which, now that I looked, didn't exactly have a door to it.

Geez. Why do these things happen to me?

Not only did I have to deal with the fact of my untimely death looming over my head and possibly around the next corner, but I also had to deal with a love triangle.

"Why did you do that?" Piper asked Chloe, who was smiling down at me.

"Because I think I love him," Chloe said.

"Here's a great idea," I said, sitting back up with much

effort. "Why don't we put this little awkward conversation on hold and resume it after we save the world?"

"You think?" Piper said, her arms crossed while she completely ignored my idea and me as well, actually.

Chloe turned then, facing Piper. "What do you want me to say?"

Piper shrugged. "I just thought that if you planned on taking him from me you should at least know for sure," she said, her voice low and almost menacing.

"I wasn't planning on taking him," Chloe said, crossing her arms. Piper's face was a tad vague when she studied the Russian girl. I had a sudden vision of the two of them entangled in a ball of claws and hair on the floor and panicked.

"Say, guys," I tried again, "can we just talk about this?"

Before anyone could say another word, the machine above me beeped loudly twice and the restraints on my leg unclasped, making a hissing sound. "It's finished," Chloe said. "Try and walk."

Swinging my legs off the gurney, I lowered my bare feet to the freezing stone floor. "Wow, that's cold," I muttered before attempting my first steps on my patched-up leg.

It was amazing.

"It isn't even sore, or anything. You guys don't happen to have a pill that can cure Alzheimer's by any chance, would you?"

"So you wanted her to kiss you?" Piper asked then, totally oblivious to the fact that I was a walking miracle.

"Of course not," I said.

"You weren't exactly pulling away," Chloe threw in, leaning against the concrete wall of the small room.

"That's the most unfair statement ever, Chloe, and you know it," I said, glaring at her. "And it was, like, literally two seconds long. A motherly peck, at best."

"If you kissed your mother that way where I come from my people would have your tongue and entrails out and string them on a pole," Piper said, turning and leaving.

"Okay, I think we're losing sight of the fact that Chloe

initiated the whole kiss, here," I called after her, looking like a shirtless idiot.

"Like I said," Chloe said, holding up her hands. "You didn't pull away."

Wait a minute.

I narrowed my eyes at her. "Did you get a haircut?"

At first Chloe looked at me in confusion, but after I kept my gaze on her, she smirked and I approached her. Placing my hands firmly on her shoulders, I softly pushed her away and looked deep into those beautiful eyes of hers. The ones I'd caught myself staring at for the past week that felt like an eternity. The very eyes that almost made me melt at the times when they weren't glaring.

Except this time, after I stared at her in silence for close to twenty seconds, they looked different.

"Who are you and what have you done with Chloe?" I said quietly, absentmindedly releasing her and slowly lowering my arms. Maybe it was because of the way she carried herself or how she talked differently, like she didn't care about anything.

I couldn't believe what I was seeing.

"You're not as dumb as I first thought, although it did take you longer than I would've thought someone who knew my sister well enough should have," she said, stepping close to me again and bringing her lips close to my ear. "It's a pleasure to meet you, cutie. My name is Beck."

Chapter 34

Enter the Robocop/Skynet/Blade-Runner rip-off girl known as Beck, Chloe's twin sister.

"Imposter!" I wanted to shout. "Fiend!" I wanted to scream. But instead the only words I found myself saying were, "You're a lousy kisser."

"Wow, you really singed my hair with that one," Beck said with exaggeration.

"Did Piper know that you were a fraud?" I asked, crossing to the doorway Piper had left not a minute ago.

"Who?" she asked, looking puzzled before saying, "Oh, the blonde girl? No, she didn't know a thing. She's even more clueless than you are."

I turned back around and was about to start a tirade of insults when I stopped.

I'd just kissed a robot.

Smiling, because she saw I was looking at her more closely now, she said, "Chloe tell you about me?"

I wasn't about to let this… thing get the upper-hand in this little talk. Not on my flipping watch.

"Enough," I answered, walking around her and looking her up and down like a farmer inspecting a tractor. "Tell me, are they mass producing you yet? If so I'll take four."

This was meant to be an almost racial jab, really. I mean, I wasn't sure how comfortable she was with being, you know, a robot with a human brain and spinal column and I wasn't exactly fond of Beck right off the bat, so I wasn't worried about her feelings.

"Not yet," she said nonchalantly with a shrug. "If so we'd have already won this war. But we're taking donations."

"If I'm going to make a contribution, can I please make a request for a newer model that doesn't have a mouth? That would take care of your atrocious kissing and your annoying voice in one shot."

Letting air hiss through her teeth, Beck grimaced at me like I'd just asked for a soda that she was out of. "Ooh, that might be hard to get past the board, sweetie. Mostly because they've discovered, through loads of tests, that only imbeciles are annoyed by my voice. Sorry."

"Too bad," I countered with a sigh. "I really could've used a few mute, mindless robots around the house."

"You might try your friend Piper. I bet we could make a few more of her, if you want."

"Nah, she wouldn't work. She's too good of a kisser," I said, looking perplexed as I put my hands on my hips. The problem I was having was she looked just like her flipping sister, so I couldn't insult her looks. Stupid twin.

"If you're wanting bad kissing and mindless we could always try and make a few more of you. Except surely God wouldn't allow more than one of your species to run about unchained on the planet."

I was losing. I knew it. But then I thought of something. Something Chloe has jumped down my throat about an eternity ago.

"If you're referring to Americans, then I'm guilty as charged," I said, holding my hands up. "This one time we had a leader that was such an idiot that he got drunk, fired off a nuke and totally screwed up the world," then I feigned surprise and said, "Oh, wait, sorry, that was one of your leaders, wasn't it? Look at me getting my history all jumbled up."

Beck's smirk almost, almost faltered and her left eye faintly twitched.

Bingo.

"Unfortunate," Beck said calmly. "If that hadn't happened then you wouldn't be losing a battle of wits right now."

"And you might still be a human being," I said, matching her same tone. "I guess since you aren't it's unfair of me to call you a bad kisser."

"That's fine, Jericho," Beck said in a friendly, forgiving way. Then she lowered her voice to a sort of loud whisper and said, with a hand close to her mouth to feign a clandestine exchange, "I know if I was about to die I'd be a tad cranky, too."

And that's when I lost the bout with Beck.

It just occurred to me that since I'm telling this to you I could've left this little conversation out of the tale as it doesn't, uh, you know, progress any of the story.

Curses.

When I didn't respond fast enough Beck winked at me and patted my shoulder. "It's alright, Jericho. I'll make sure they make what's left of you into a mindless robot like me," she said, walking past me. "Maybe even one without a mouth."

I turned to watch her walk away and saw Chloe standing in the doorway. "You're awake," she said.

"I think he may have suffered a brain injury, sis. He seems to think he's a good kisser," Beck said, passing her sister without any further explanation. I also noticed that Chloe wasn't exactly exchanging fist bumps, so I was thinking that she and Beck weren't being very sisterly since their reunion. It was also crazy to see them next to each other since they were both wearing the same black jumpsuit. Once she was well away from us Chloe approached me.

"Are you hurting anywhere?" she asked.

"Just my pride," I muttered, sitting back on the gurney. "Your sister is a real charmer. What was she like as a child?"

"Shorter," Chloe confirmed, crossing to me. "Perhaps slightly less bitter."

"Getting blown to smithereens will do that to a girl, they tell me," I said. "She pretended to be you when I woke up. Why was she even there to begin with?"

Chloe shrugged. "Piper and I were beat, Jericho. She must've wanted to take a look at you while we were asleep."

"She kissed me," I said, not really wanting to accept Chloe's shrug for some reason. "Rubbed on my chest and Piper thinks you're trying to steal me from her and you just shrug?" I couldn't help it. I was a tad upset.

Again, Chloe shrugged. "She's been me for years, Jericho. I can't tell her who she can or can't kiss," then she glanced sideways at me. "Although I have to say that I'm a tad jealous she beat me to it," she said, elbowing my shoulder softly.

"Don't worry, Chloe," I told her. "Apparently, I'm a bad kisser, anyway, so you aren't missing anything."

It did kind of stink, really, if you think about it. Here I am with two amazing female protagonists with me for most of the story and the first kiss goes to the evil robot-chick.

Chloe's smile faltered, and she suddenly touched my arm. "Jericho, I know you've got too much on your plate, but you should know that Beck isn't the way she used to be in more ways than her body. She's the leader of the Rebels now and she's also dangerous."

I frowned. "How dangerous?"

"Very," Chloe said. I hadn't seen her this shook up since she explained to me about her father's safety ages ago. "They've had clinical tests on subjects to try and make something like Beck for a-hundred years or more. The reason it was deemed illegal over twenty years ago was because the subjects all ended up with the same results or side-effects."

"Like being extremely obnoxious?" I asked.

"Try the human brain completely rejecting the process of robotics being grafted to the spine," she said. "Once that was discovered scientists found out that by simply isolating and removing a single brain cell in the left frontal lobe, a secure binding could be achieved."

"And that was the brain cell that made people not be obnoxious?"

"I suppose you could look at it that way. Side-effects aren't visible right away but over time the cell will try and grow back and sometime during that process the subjects became removed from themselves as well as other's around them."

"So they, like, start feeling crazy?"

"They start feeling human again and that causes the

conflict. Regardless of how many times the greatest minds of our generation have tried and retried, the end result was always a reclusive, violent person with a lot of expensive hardware inside of them that ended up being disposed of."

I looked at her. "Disposed of? Like, killed?"

Nodding, she said, "That's when they outlawed it."

"So your sister's problem is what?"

"She's still alive," Chloe said quietly. "Beck is my sister, Jericho. But that doesn't change the fact that she wasn't supposed to be like this. No one is. That's the reason the cell grows back in the first place. The brain knows that the spine is being violated and it tries to purge it."

This was a lot to take in. "Beck could snap at any time and start, like, killing people?"

"The cell normally grows back in a few months, so she's already snapped. That and her memory returning were most likely the reasons she ran away again," Chloe said.

"But Beck isn't reclusive," I told her. "If anything, she's the exact opposite. And I can vouch for her knowledge of the witticism dictionary personally."

"That's where I draw a blank," Chloe said, shaking her head slightly. "All previous tests were done in a controlled lab with simulated scenarios at best, so there isn't any data on how people like Beck would react to the real world."

"Well, she runs things around here, so I guess she's reacting pretty well," I stood up straight and stretched. "A group of rebels screaming, shouting, and fighting for equality in the world might be just the thing a person who feels non-human might need."

"Maybe," Chloe said and then we were silent for what seemed like a long time. Then she asked, "Was Piper angry?"

I nodded. "Yeah."

"You don't have to worry about me getting in your way, Jericho. I've seen the way you look at her."

"Appreciate it," I muttered. "Now if we could only get the D batteries out of your sister's back, I'd be at the top again."

Chloe laughed at that before getting serious again and saying, "Please don't say anything like that to Beck. I'm not sure how stable she is so you might want to lay off the synthetic jokes and comments."

Uh oh.

"So, what'd the two of you talk about?" Chloe asked.

Shrugging, I began walking the direction Piper had gone and she fell in step behind me.

"Nothing."

Chapter 35

"So you didn't kiss Jericho?" Piper asked Chloe after the two of us had found her in the dingy, hard room that the Rebels had given to her. Chloe explained what had happened.

"No," Chloe confirmed. "Although the thought has crossed my mind," she added with a smile. "Only he doesn't look like he'd be the best kisser, if I had to assume."

It took Piper about three full seconds for the story to sink in, her to be cool with it and then for her to realize that Beck had mega played her and then she was mad. "Who does she think she is?" Piper asked.

I listened again to Beck's not-so-easy-on-the-ears back story as Chloe once again related the tale to Piper. Not sure why she felt the need to explain things to the Viking girl, considering Piper had long since given up trying to understand the future.

When Chloe finished, Piper said, "A renowned man in our village once killed a mother bear in a cave but kept her cub alive and brought it home. It was fun and cute when it was small and on a rope, but as it grew it became dangerous and bloodthirsty as a bear should be. Then it had to be killed."

This wasn't what Chloe wanted to hear but it also wasn't anything she hadn't already thought of, I could tell. "She's like this because her team came up against mine in a firefight and mine won. I've already killed her once and I'm not exactly standing in line to do it again, if I can help it."

"Well, I'm glad you got that off your chest." Beck said.

What the heck? Where did she come from? Whirling around like fifth graders caught with a cigarette lighter, we all looked at her leaning against the doorframe with her arms crossed.

"Don't worry, sister. Words can't explain how little I fear you, so I'm not worried about whether or not you intend to put down your bear-like sibling," then she entered the room and nodded at Piper. "Good metaphor, by the way. Think that up all by yourself?"

Before Beck could say anything else hurtful to anyone, I said, "You run the show, Beck. When are we going for Klaus?"

"Look at you all eager to die," Beck said, flopping onto the ragged couch in the room. Leaning back into the almost nonexistent cushion on the sofas back, she crossed her legs and extended a hand to me. "Sit with me, Jericho."

"I'd rather stand, if it's all the same to you."

"It is all the same to me and I'd prefer you sit."

"Go to Helheim," Piper said, taking a step in Beck's direction.

Beck laughed at that. It was a goodhearted chuckle really, the way someone might chuckle when playing a laid-back fun game of foosball with a few friends.

Not the way someone normal chuckles at a hardened Viking girl with more than a few kills under her belt.

"You three are a tiresome lot," Beck said and almost yawned. "Just sit, Jericho. I really don't bite no matter how bearish you might think I am."

Since I wasn't exactly ready for another round of wit warfare, I sat beside her. "See?" she asked, smiling and linking her arm through mine. "How hard was that?"

"Just tell me your plan," I said, shifting uncomfortably beside her.

Shrugging, Beck said, "There really isn't much to it, really. I could've killed Klaus long ago but never had a reason to."

"How about saving the world?"

No sooner had the words left my mouth than Beck's inhuman eyes flicked to mine and all traces of jokes and laughter vanished.

I know this sounds crazy, but my heart also skipped a beat when the she locked her gaze on me.

And not in a good way.

Leaning toward me slightly, Beck's eyes never left mine

while her arm tightened around mine and she said, "Do you really think that I care what happens to this world?"

Not wanting her to realize I was almost crazy scared, I said, "I'm going to go with no but, if that's so, why help us?"

Beck leaned back again. She didn't look positively demonic like she had just looked, but she wasn't playing around anymore for some reason. I know this is a tad unimportant now but I really didn't understand why, after all the trash talk she and I exchanged, did she decide to go all crazy on me when I asked her about saving the world.

I mean, not to put too much of a point on it but, hey, it's only saving the world, after all, right?

"Although you're all tiresome, I can't help but be intrigued by your little suicide mission," pulling me backward, she clasped my hand between hers and said, in a manner that an older sister would explain something to a younger sibling, "You see, Jericho, although Klaus has never given me a reason to kill him I must confess that his knowledge of me is most unsettling."

I frowned. "What would that matter?"

"Klaus was the head of the research teams twenty years ago," Chloe told me. "He'd love to get his hands on someone like Beck."

"Now *you* don't have to feel bad for wanting me," Beck said, smiling "I'm in high demand, you see."

It was hard not to say something along the lines of, "Oh yeah? Are the newer models going to be bug free and not have as many mental issues?"

It was so hard to not say, in fact, that I, uh, might have actually said it. Just kind of slipped out.

Beck's smile broadened. "He's so cute. I'll take four," then she sighed and stood. "On a serious note, Klaus just wants me so he can dissect my body and find out what makes me tick."

She glanced at me after a few seconds of silence and said, "What? No snappy comeback? There might be hope for you yet."

Not being able to help myself yet again, I asked, "Didn't you leave the first time for some Rebel Romeo dude? I'd love to meet this guy because obviously his brain would be a great contribution to science in their studies of complete idiots, while we're talking about dissecting, I mean."

"Jericho—" Chloe began but Beck held up a hand, cutting her off.

"His name was Devlin," she said. "And you're a few years late for a meeting, I'm afraid. I killed him a long time ago. If you find his body, though, let me know. He had a nice pair of boots on when I broke his neck and tossed him off a bridge."

I guess I must've been the only person in the room with shock on my face because Beck laughed out loud big time when she saw my expression. "I took his spot as the leader and he must not have liked that because I found out he was selling information to the Bears," shrugging, she added. "Plus he was a terrible kisser."

"Sorry I asked," I muttered. "You're tough, scary and a little on the crazy side of things. I think we've all established that. Now can we please get back to Klaus?"

"His makeshift presidium is fifty stories above us and a few blocks down the street," Beck said simply, and all four of us glanced at the ceiling for some reason. "We've found the entrance to the lower levels of his building but never went into it because, like I said, we never had a reason to."

"So we won't know what's on the other side," Piper said.

"Oh, I could think of a few things that would probably be there to greet us and none of them are good, honey," Beck told her while sitting on the arm of the mutilated couch. "And the firepower we'd need to fight back with won't fit through the backdoor, so to speak."

We were all silent while we hashed out different plans in our heads. I mean, I know that's what I was doing, anyway. Not exactly about getting into Klaus's facility, but more so what the Helheim we were going to do when we actually found him.

Klaus was no doubt getting ready with his plan, but I kept reminding myself that we had the final piece of his evil puzzle with us. He couldn't finish his scheme without the original gauntlet. As if she were reading my mind, Beck said, "I would advise leaving the glove here, Jericho."

I was a little disconcerted at the mentioning of what I was thinking and glanced at her. She was watching me closely. Wait. She wasn't really reading my mind, was she?

Not a flipping chance in Helheim. I thought, to see if she was really in my head.

Smiling, she said, "You know it's not a good idea to have it with you when confronting Klaus."

"I also know that it's not a good idea to leave it in the hands of you and your pals. Sorry, but I can only handle one psycho time-traveling overlord at a time, thank you," I know Chloe had warned me to lay off, but Beck wasn't exactly giving me the best material to work with on being polite.

Beck shrugged. "Have it your way. I hope I'm close by to tell you I told you so," then she addressed Chloe. "When do you want to do this suicide mission?"

Suicide. The word was meant to apply to everyone going on the said mission, except everyone going all knew that the only suicide certain was mine.

Then I saw that they were all looking at me for a decision. "What's the rush?" I wanted to say. "We got his port key so why hurry off to my death?"

Except I didn't say that.

I simply said a sophisticated version of it.

"I'm not ready to die yet, guys," I told them all. "I think I'm going to take a bit to, like, think about a few things first."

Incidentally that's when I decided to verbally record what you're hearing right now on the gauntlet. I'm not sure what good it'll be but I just had to tell someone. So thanks for listening, whoever-you-are.

"Craven," Beck said, crossing her arms. "Death isn't so bad the first time around so long as your dear sister uses explosive rounds causing instant third-degree burns. Then you won't feel a thing while you die," then she smiled at Chloe. "Thanks for that, by the way."

"You're welcome," Chloe snapped. I guess even she'd had enough of Beck's mouth. "What makes you think I wanted to kill you?"

"Oh, no doubt you were just following the rules like the good little soldier you always were."

"And you were breaking them like the good little rebel you always were and you paid dearly for it," Chloe said, her voice rising.

"Did I?" Beck asked her menacingly and then they were in each other's faces.

That's when I left. I didn't know where I was going or why, but I just couldn't hear squabbling sisters right then. The underground went on forever, it felt like, as I trudged along, passing lots of people with smudges of grease on their faces and guns in their hands.

Eventually I must've gone in a circle, or something, because I ended up close to the room I'd woke up in. Hours had passed by already during my walk around the Rebel base, and since I figured I didn't have anything better to do, I entered the medical room with the notion of lying my soon-to-be deceased body on the rather uncomfortable gurney and at least get a good night's sleep before I died the next day.

Except when I laid down I couldn't sleep. Like, at all. After tossing and turning on the ragged gurney for about ten minutes I sat up.

And that's when I decided to record my story.

I stood and crossed the room to the nightstand, the only other piece of furniture in the room besides the one chair beside the gurney, and I picked up the gauntlet of time. Sitting in the chair I put the glove on, flipped through the touchscreen and found the recording section.

I guess this was originally added to the glove for a no doubt intrepid explorer to verbally record their many journeys through time.

"I might be dead in a few hours," I started off. "Please, I don't need your pity, sympathy or any other means of..." I talked for a good two minutes or so and stopped right before I started talking about the Vikings because my thoughts turned to Piper.

I stopped the recording and stood up suddenly.

I had a few things left to do before I delved into my tale.

Chapter 36

It didn't take me long to find Piper. She ended up being in the same room I'd left her in, only Beck and Chloe were nowhere to be seen. Which was great, let me tell you.

"Jericho," she said, smiling warmly at me when I entered the dim room, "are you well?"

I'd tried to work up a good way to put the thoughts in my head. Here, check out what it sounded like in my mind.

"Piper, I just want you to know that I'm scared. I've tried to be tough this whole time but now that I'm staring death in the face, I must confess I'm hesitant. The world as we know it depends on me facing Klaus and maybe dying in the process. I don't want you to go with me because I'm afraid you'll die, too. I want you to make it back to your village and live the rest of your life not having to worry about things that don't even apply to you or your time."

Yeah, that's what it sounded like in my mind.

What I ended up saying was, "So you really like me, huh?"

She nodded.

Crossing over to her, I pulled her up to me and brushed a strand of her blonde hair out of her face. "This is for just in case I die tomorrow," I said, holding the back of her head and planting a one-of-a-kind, bodacious, classic Jericho Johnson kiss on her lips.

Okay, in all honesty I'm not a very good kisser. I've been told that on multiple occasions. Guess being rich cancelled that little thing out. But now I was kissing someone who didn't care about my fortune and when I pulled back I was already regretting my decision to—

Then she kissed me.

I'm not sure how long it lasted because, frankly, I didn't have a stopwatch on hand and don't really feel the need to explain the length of kissing to you.

After another hour with the warrior woman of my dreams, which had more kissing, talking, laughing, kissing, joking, kissing, more laughing, more talking and yes, more kissing in it, I stood.

"I'm going back to the med bay," I told her. "There's something I have to finish up."

"Must you?"

Smiling, I brushed my knuckles across her cheek. "Yeah. This is kind of important. But I'll see you tomorrow, and if I don't die the day after tomorrow, too."

If you haven't already deduced that I left the hot Viking chick of my dreams to come sit in a dusty, dark room and record this story for you, then I'll go ahead and say it for you.

I left a hot Viking woman of my dreams to come sit in a dusty, dark room alone to record this story for you, whoever-you-are.

So if we ever meet up one day, you owe me a coffee.

On my way back to my uncomfortable gurney, I ran into Beck on the catwalk. Well, I actually didn't run into her. She was standing in my way with her arms folded, so I had to stop when I reached her.

"Evening," I said to her. "Beautiful night, isn't it?"

"It's 10 in the morning," she told me, rolling her eyes.

"We're underground. Forgive me for not keeping my sundial on hand."

I tried to step past her, but she put a hand firmly on my chest. "Look, I know you don't want to die, and all, but the best time to crash Klaus's party is in about nine hours from now. He only comes to his facility twice a week, and if we don't act now you'll have to wait till after the weekend and I don't think I can stand to look at your depressed face that long."

"Noted," I said, stepping back and folding my arms. "So, what, we just kick down the back door and start shooting folks?"

"Infiltrating has its pros and cons. The cons outweigh the pros by a long shot, so I think I got a better idea," she said, turning. "Walk with me."

"Geez, but you sure do love telling people what to do," I said, falling in step behind her. The production lines had ceased working below us, so the only noise really was the sound of our resounding footsteps on the catwalk. I noticed that my Chucks didn't look near as intimidating as Beck's heeled leather boots.

"Where's Chloe?" I asked.

"I'm not sure. She left after our discussion and I haven't seen her since," we walked the rest of the way to the med bay in silence. Once I was seated in the only chair, Beck explained her new plan.

"I can arrange a diversion topside in front of his building when he's on his way out. He won't notice anyone important after having to deal with hundreds of rioters," she said.

Riot.

"Would a passing scientist maybe mistake your riot for a revolt?" I asked.

Beck frowned. "I suppose he might due to what's been going on lately up there."

"And is Klaus's building located in the southern precinct?"

Beck narrowed her eyes at me and answered, "Yes. Why?"

"Just curious," I told her as Atrium Sparks' recollection of my demise rang throughout my brain. "Sounds good. I'll kill Klaus while you guys distract his guards and we'll be good to go," standing, I held out a hand to her. "I appreciate all you're doing. Even if you're only doing it so you won't have to look at my depressing face for a whole weekend."

Beck accepted my hand before pulling me toward her suddenly hard and covering my lips with hers roughly.

Before you start thinking of how I was a backstabbing heart-breaker, let me stop you right there and say that I wasn't expecting crazy girl to kiss me again while holding the front of my shirt like a bully might a kid he was about to beat up. It wasn't a long kiss, thank God, and after she released me she took a step back, put one hand on her hip and looked at me.

"What the heck was that?" I asked in agitation, touching

my lip and seeing a little blood on my fingers.

"Just checking if I still thought you were a bad kisser."

"And?" I replied curtly, spitting blood on the concrete floor.

"Nope," said Beck as she turned to the doorway. "You're still horrible at it."

"So just bite my flipping bottom lip off, then," I said loudly as she exited the room.

So, after yet another fun encounter with Beck, I laid down on the gurney and picked my story up where I left off. Now you're pretty much up to speed, whoever-you-are. You know everything I know.

I keep wanting to have this, like, amazing conclusion to all of this and actually wanted to wait until after I'd saved the world to record it but didn't want to risk, you know, dying and no one getting to hear any of it.

I figure ninety-eight percent of a story is better than none at all when time-travel is involved.

Tomorrow I'm going to face Klaus in the freezing streets of Flagstaff, so I guess I'll see what happens in about nine hours.

I'm going to sleep now before I hyperventilate.

With any luck, I might even get to talk to you after my dance with death.

Peace out, whoever-you-are, and don't forget that even if I die in a few hours—

I'm still awesome.

Epilogue

Dr. Cross was leaning back in his desk chair with his fingers laced behind his head when the recording ended. He sat like that for a while afterward, lost in thought.

Klaus had indeed been killed not six hours ago by the very explosion that almost killed Jericho Johnson. Standing, the doctor crossed to thick window and once again peered out over Flagstaff.

Klaus wasn't the only collateral damage from the bombing. Chloe Sparks had also been killed. Beck and the Viking girl hadn't been accounted for yet, but it wouldn't surprise him if reports came soon of their bodies being found in the rubble of what was left of the southern precinct.

"Ritu, report," he said suddenly, and the nurse's face materialized on the window.

"He's dying," was all she said.

"How long left?" Dr. Cross asked, walking quickly to his door and exiting. The image of Ritu followed him down the hallway on the plexiglass walls as he jogged to the elevator. "Minutes, sir. We've tried everything, but his body is still rejecting all of our medications."

"He can't die," he told her, pushing a button as the elevator descended at an alarming rate to the bottom level of his building. "He mustn't."

When the doors opened he stepped out and jogged to the end of the hallway, entering the door on his right. Ritu was standing beside the bed with a few other white-coated men and they instantly moved out of Cross's way.

Dr. Cross peered down at the man he now knew so much about.

Or what was left of him.

His right arm was gone from the elbow down, most of

his hair had been burned off and he was missing an eye. Not to mention that every inch of him was covered in horribly grotesque burns. The only things keeping him alive were the needles riddled over his mutilated body pumping medications inside of him and an oxygen tube that normally would've went down a patient's throat but was running through a gaping hole in the chest to his lungs.

Then the corpse in front of him screamed and tried to sit up.

"Hold him," Cross shouted, putting his hands on the shaking man's shoulders and feeling the heat from the burns instantly. One eye locked on Cross as the other two men helped him shove the thrashing man down. "Sedation," Dr. Cross shouted again. "Now!"

Ritu hit a few keys on the holodesk beside the bed and in seconds the screams turned to moans then his only eye closed.

Cross cursed when the heart rate monitor flat lined. Running to one side of the lab he tore into a cabinet and in seconds found what he needed. Rushing back to the now dead man, he stabbed the adrenal shot hard through his burned chest and into his heart.

The next scream to escape the parched throat was positively primeval and ear-splitting. The screams only lasted a minute after that before he lost consciousness. His heart rate wasn't the best Cross had seen on a holograph but at least there was a heart rate.

"Dr. Cross," Ritu said from behind him, "I've never questioned your reasons behind anything, but this man is suffering the worst of pain. I don't know who he is but—"

"His name is Jericho Johnson," Cross said while washing the charred flesh from his hands and forearms at a sink in the room. "His body, although a little worse for wear, is a perfect host for Z-90. I want him in the Phoenix program."

"Z-90 doesn't work," Ritu said blatantly. "And the Phoenix program—"

"Enough," he said, watching the brown water swirl down

the drain before turning back to her. "And I'll say it again. He can't die."

"Why?" Ritu asked, perplexed.

Dr. Cross glanced back over Jericho's completely burned body.

A left index finger moved slightly.

Cross smiled. "Because he's not done yet."

End of Book One of The Phoenix Cycle